Who BeCharlie B.

G. K. Fralin

ISBN: **1495236129**
ISBN-13**978-1495236129**:

DEDICATION
For all the Charlie's who for whatever reason suffer prejudice; take strength in who you are.

CONTENTS

ACKNOWLEDGMENTS

Editing Assistant: Faith Colburn
Micheal Eaken cover design

Victorine Lieske cover title and shading.

Wymore Public Library

People of Wymore for their stories about the orignal Charlie

Laughlin Hoevet Funeral Home

Georgia Friese

Evelyn Jackson for her memories of her Uncle Charlie

Karolyn Riemann

Chapter 1: 1905 Father Dies

"Boy, you can't sit up here! Niggers don't get a seat. You stand in the back. When the service is over, you get the family's wagon and drive them to the cemetery." The words burst like a venomous whisper from the funeral director's mouth, and nobody would question his dismay except the mother of the young man the insult targeted.

Brown skinned, twenty year old Charlie Bueller stood next to his white mother listening, unable to defend himself, for to do so would make the situation worse.

"Pardon me sir but this man is not a nigger. This is my son Charlie and that is his father in the casket." Lula Bueller's eyes shot fire straight into those of the offender as she tipped her head toward the coffin that held her husband. "Now, we've traveled back here from Wyman to bury my husband, his father. I'd appreciate a little respect."

"Madam, I respect that the man in the coffin is your husband, and this may be your son, but he is certainly not the son of the man in that coffin. I don't know what goes on in Wyman, but this is Blue Rivers and we don't mix the two."

Charlie wanted to jump to this mother's defense, but he couldn't, not here.

"Sir, do not insult me or my son." Her whisper became tight and menacing. "I do not care what you believe. My son will sit with me."

"Then you will both sit in the back pew."

Charlie's light brown skin turned rust as heat rose to his face from anger and embarrassment; anger at a man who disrespected his mother, embarrassment that he was the cause. A discreet scan around the room at pinched faces glaring back didn't help, His only hope was to get through it. *Why do I feel I'm disgracing my own father's funeral?*

Lula Bueller never allowed a man to best her when she vented righteous indignation. However, for once the son was proud his mother relented for the sake of decorum. Shoulders squared, she motioned her other children ranging from eighteen year old George to three year old Pearl resting on the hip of her sister. Six of the children obediently followed.

George stayed with his Grandparents.

"Mother, please stay in front for pa. Please. I don't mind sitting in the back."

"Not now son." She put a finger to her lips and the matter was no longer open for discussion.

When they reached the back row of pews, she put her arm out to stop him and motioned the other Bueller children into the pew after which she sat. The oldest Bueller son, to his horror, now sat in the seat taken by the head of a family. The stares from guests seemed to bare his dark body. Charlie let his face go blank the way pa taught him in poker. The workmanship of the room suited for temporary distraction. Charlie looked at the high polished, cherry wood trim of the windows and doors repeated in the crown molding. *The ceiling to floor, dark blue, velvet drapes must have cost a fortune. The only thing that makes more money than saloons must be mortuaries*

The people in the room whispered just a little too loudly as they managed multiple glances in Charlie direction. The young man wanted to stand in the back; "in his proper place", but wouldn't do that to his mother. The only recourse was to allow his mind to fly back to his boyhood, to a time when there was no doubt of his station in life.

***

"Pa, can I come to Wyman with you?" Charlie craned his twelve year old neck looking up to his hero.

"I'm planning on it. I'm going to work you hard building the new place." Henry looked at his oldest son and then to his second son "You too Georgie."

The boon of the railroad in Wyman gave Henry Bueller the idea to move and open a boarding house there. He rode the train from Marysville to Wyman and bought a large plot near the downtown area. The old boarding house in Blue Rivers would sell soon enough.

Henry returned home to load a large wagon with tools and his two oldest sons. On reaching what would be their new home Henry proclaimed, "Boys the Bueller family is going to prosper and grow here."

On his first visit to Wyman, Henry had met and befriended Dr. and Mrs. Wilson from across the street of the new construction. Within four months the three men, with the help of some neighbors Dr. Wilson recruited, had, framed a house five rooms long, two rooms deep and two full stories tall. Winter wasn't far off. They finished the outside, painted the siding, shingled the roof and framed the interior walls. What remained would be completed with the family in residence.

Henry had one last project before returning to Blue Rivers, Kansas to gather the family for the move to Wyman. "Boys, the front door needs a shingle. What shall it say?"

"Bueller Boarding House on one line," George offered.

"Established 1897 on the second line," Charlie finished.

"Perfect! Bueller Boarding House, Established 1897. Charlie, established is a big word for such a young lad. Where did you learn a big word like that?"

"Pa, you know Ma teaches us all our lessons. Figures and vocabulary are most important she says. Besides, I saw the word on the shingle of our own boarding house in Blue Rivers."

"Got me didn't you?" Henry Bueller patted his oldest son on the back. Then the father gave equal attention to George. "Both of my sons talk with fanciful words."

Henry constructed and hung the shingle then made a sign OPENING SOON that hung above it.

A large, lavish hotel went up much closer to the depot. The hotel didn't really threaten the success of the Bueller Boarding House. The two establishments did not seek the same clientele. The plan was to build a home with extra rooms for rent to long term boarders, possibly railroad workers.

During the eight years since moving to Wyman, the family had flourished.

Lula was a brilliant cook. She kept her noon table open to anyone who wanted to come in for a meal at no charge. Guests filled the huge dining table. The meal served as good will. Guests often brought supplies from their own farms and gardens to help fill the pots. The evening meal was strictly for family and boarders.

***

Now, Charlie wondered if anyone of the men who helped them build the boarding house had known he was a Bueller, or had they just accepted he was a young black boy the Bueller's took in? Did it matter, he knew most of Wyman was aware of his identity.

The hum of the room made Charlie's attention return to more people filling the chapel. Most of them he didn't know. Eight years had passed since they left Blue Rivers, for Wyman. He counted twenty people in attendance when the director closed the doors to the room. The railroad superintendent from Wyman showed up to pay respects for a man who died working for the railroad. The rest were likely distant cousins, and friends of his grandparents. The grandparents from both the Bueller and Volker sides sat in the front row looking back to see where their family was. Charlie knew they had witnessed the exchange between the funeral director and his mother. Then his Grandma Bueller turned to look in his direction and blew him a kiss.

A gasp went up from several people in the room as if his grandmother had also broken some cardinal rule. *Why can't they just have some respect for Pa and his family? At least, they could feel sorry for the white part of the family.* Then he smiled. *I guess Grandma got the reaction she was looking for. The women in my life are too brave for their own good."* A grin crept across his mouth.

Many times over the years, Charlie felt the effects of his coloring even with all his parents' protection. However, until that day he'd never felt so on display because of it. He hung his head and held his left hand over the side of his face. His mother grasped his right arm.

"Son, you put that hand in your lap. It is your father in that coffin. You have no shame. Ignore the fools.

Charlie had no desire to disappoint his mother. He felt like a boy trying to hide under his bed. The idea of heading a household in his father's stead sickened him. With his hands in his lap, there seemed only one way of escape and that was to let his mind go back in time. He swallowed and made his face blank.

The attempt to retreat into the boy with the dusty ball, tossing it back and forth to his brother evaded him. Instead, the day of blood and creosote flowed back like a rush of ripping torment throbbing in his skull.

***

Charlie worked inside the railroad station sweeping. He smiled at the way his father joked with the passengers who waited to board the oncoming train. Henry spent his days signaling the train conductors and loading passengers' baggage. That cheerful chatter with the passengers was a bonus.

That last day, a scream ripped through the depot as passengers backed into the station house. The spine bending screech of metal on metal mixed into the noise. Charlie's breath caught, but he could not see past the mass of bodies. Mrs. Wilson looked his direction and pointed out the door.

"Pa?"

One look at her face of tears told Charlie it was indeed his father. .

He pushed through the bedlam to the platform. People pointed to the tracks. There his father lay on the rails under the engine. The brakeman ran to the front and waved the engine to back up. Henry Bueller's body ripped as he screamed in agony.

Charles jumped on the tracks hoping his father's wounds would be superficial, but Henry's chest fought to move air in and out. Instead, blood gushed out of his ripped and torn body, crushed under the weight of the engine while he gurgled red drops from his mouth.

Henry mouthed two words, "My son."

Two men slid a board under the now limp body and carried it to the platform. The would be passengers shied away. "Didn't you see the man wanted his son?" The shocked brakeman yelled. "He wanted his son."

Mrs. Wilson slid up to the man. "That is his son." Charles was still in earshot and warmed toward lady with salt and pepper hair.

***

"Charlie, are you with us?" He felt a tug on his sleeve.

"Oh," he jumped slightly, "yes ma my mind wandered off a bit." He noticed everyone was standing as the organist played chords of "Just as I Am" He could not resist singing out with his full baritone.

The minister's benediction ended the service and soon the burial at the cemetery sealed the finality of a man's life. The goodbye was all too short for the great Henry Bueller. The oldest son regretted his lack of attention through the service. Pa deserved better.

"Charlie," a demanding five year old tugged at his leg. "Pick me up, I'm cold."

"Okey Dokey Early B. up you go." Charlie hoisted his youngest brother over his head onto his shoulders. He buried the youngsters feet under his bulky, wool covered arms. The boy reached his hands under Charlie's coat collar. Ma carried little Pearl. The large Bueller family loaded the wagon and slowly clip clopped out of the cemetery and back to Blue Rivers.

Grandma and Grandpa Bueller hosted the family and friend

remembrance dinner, served buffet style, with more dishes than would fit on the large sideboard. The women of the Blue Rivers Methodist Church took over the kitchen keeping the plates, and silver clean and stacked.

Charlie filled his plate and looked for a place he could be alone. Ultimately, he went out on the screened back porch and stood eating his meal. He didn't taste much of it, but his belly was full.

"Young man, I have been looking for you!" Grandpa Bueller stepped out onto the wooden porch. "You're going to freeze out here."

"I'm sorry Grandpa. I needed a place to get away for a bit."

"Me too son, me too"

Tears filled Charlie's eyes. "They wouldn't let me sit up front. Ma got mad and made all the kids sit with us in the back. She gave up her place for me, Grandpa. I told her to stay with you all, but she wouldn't have it."

"Charlie, your mother did exactly as your father would have had her do. Do you ever remember your pa letting anyone insult you around him?"

"No, he and ma have always been strong on that." He tried to impersonate his father's voice. "Charlie, why is that noggin of yours hanging low? Pull it up high over those shoulders."

They both laughed. "Not bad, you sound like him."

The men talked on that porch until it was too dark to see. When the light blinked off and on, they knew to go inside.

"You stood out there over an hour. You should be freezing. Neither one of you had the sense to put on your coat." Grandma Bueller grabbed small chair quilts and gave them a fierce rub.

Lula offered them coffee. "We'd love it when grandma quits shaking us like rag dolls."

Grandma Bueller let them go. The old man's thin, gray hair fluffed like a ruffled cat. Charlie and Lula laughed as Charlie held his hands up by his head with fingers splayed. Grandpa looked at his reflection in the bottom of a pan and laughed at his disheveled hair.

"Well Charlie, that's one thing you don't have a problem with."

They all laughed and for the first time that day, Charlie didn't feel ashamed.

Most guests left an hour earlier. The rest of the Bueller children followed the Grandparents Volker into the kitchen.

The group laughed even louder when Grandpa Volker asked. "What the heck is going on in here?"

Lula looked at her parents and then pointed to Grandpa Bueller's hair still uncombed.

"I see." The puzzled look remained on Grandpa Volker's face as Grandma Volker started laughing at the scene. "You're all nuts." Mr.

Volker sounded his ruling.

"Father, it's been a long day, we found something to laugh at, and I must say I'm feeling much better for it." Lula replied.

Grandpa Volker kissed Lula on the cheek. "If it makes you feel better, I'm all for it dear." He smiled and waved for Grandma Volker. "Ma, I think we had better head home. In this cold, I am not at all sure that new car will go where I point it. I often wish we hadn't invested in the damn thing."

"Robert! Watch your language."

"Pardon me." He obediently excused himself and winked at Charlie. "Okay, who is coming to stay at our place tonight?"

George appeared from somewhere. "I'd like to go if I may. Just me, please"

"George what is wrong with you?" Lula asked her second son.

"Ma, I can't talk about it now." George squeezed the words through clenched teeth.

"It's okay dear," Grandma Bueller jumped in. "We have plenty of room for the rest of you. George may be able to help your folks if the car has problems."

"You may go, but I want an explanation when we get home." Lula warned.

The rest of the boys filled two beds in an upstairs room, while the girls slept with their mother in a second of the three bedrooms.

Jack and Roy squeezed into one bed while Fred and Earl took the other.

Charles picked up six year old Earl and swung him onto the soft mattress. "Who be Early B?"

Earl's giggle was sweet to the ears, "me, me, me. "Who be Charlie B.?"

"I be Charlie B. and I'm gonna squash you in that bed." The large man lay atop the protesting child, much of his weight held by his own arms. The youngster continued to giggle.

"Charlie dangit, I was just getting this mattress to fit."

"Sorry Fred" Charlie winked at Earl.

"Charlie, why is mommy so sad?"

"Hmm, we're all sad Early, but momma is most sad because daddy died and went to be with the angels. She's going to miss him."

"Why can't he come back? I want daddy." The young lad's voice quivered. He started to sob.

"I'm sorry. I'll be here for you and so will your other brothers. Momma is still here to take care of all of us, but we need to help her feel better and maybe that will make us feel better too."

"Okay, I'll help her. Will she feel better if I make her a letter to daddy?"

"That might just do the trick. Not yet though. We'll talk about it later."

"You boys settle down before I come in there." Lula's voice carried through the door.

"Oops, ma caught us. Shush," Charles sang a sweet lullaby.

"You do have that nice voice big brother." Roy spoke up from the other bed.

After spreading a bedroll on the floor, Charlie put his head on one of Grandma Bueller's homemade down pillows. He didn't think he would sleep, but the pillow was soft enough to overcome the day.

Chapter 2: Closed Doors

Charlie looked at the home he'd known for the first twelve years of his life. The need to find that welcome warmth again had drawn him to walk the seven blocks from his grandparent's house. The only thing different on the exterior seemed to be an intrusive sign "Blue River's Inn, Mrs. Morgan Proprietor."

A middle aged woman opened the door at his knock. "Hello Ma'am my name is Charles Bueller. My folks used to have this house, do you mind if I come in?"

"Humph, who do you think you are now? Get on yer way. Nigra's running an Inn, that's a story you can sell somewhere else.

"My folks are white ma'am. We buried my pa yesterday. May I just come in and sit for a minute?"

"I don't take yer kind into the front! How absurd, you lying to me boy. I don't like lying especially from a nigra."

A great sigh escaped Charlie as he forced calm to overrule his anger. "Could I just see the kitchen where I worked with my ma?"

"Oh, okay but not long."

"I can find my way ma'am, I lived here until" she slammed the door, "I was twelve." He finished the sentence facing a closed door. Then took a step back to study the building a moment. Someone should *do some tuck pointing on that stone. Maybe I'll suggest myself for the job and make the old bitch pay out the nose.*

The door to the back entrance seemed small. He knocked and a curt voice yelled from the interior to come in. A black man of about sixty was mixing batter for pancakes. The smell of pork sausage made Charlie's mouth water.

"Well, did ye forget to bring the milk wid ye or whatever ye be deliverin'?"

"Oh, no sir, I'm not delivering anything. I used to live here when my folks owned it back about eight years ago."

"Do tell," the cook responded shaking his head. "Tell another whopper boy. Blacks don't own businesses like this less'n they want to have an empty Inn." The cook looked up from his batter. "Why ye talkin' all high n' mighty nigga?"

"My parents aren't black. I'm the oldest of the Bueller children. I'm sorry if the way I talk upsets you sir. My mother insisted on proper speech and manners."

"You jist tone 'er down there boy. This be my kitchen. I heard they had them a black baby. She fooled around somewhere. Some people think it were me. I weren't here then. The widder lady hired me after they were gone."

"Excuse me, but that is my mother you are speaking of. I am as much Henry Bueller's son as I am hers. They made sure I knew that."

"Sure son, I didn't mean to say any disrespect of yer mama." The man's eyes rolled back in their sockets.

Charlie retreated through the back door and stalked the alleys to his grandparent's house. When he got there, he stood on the screened back porch huffing to catch his breath and to calm his anger. His rage gave way and he took his balled up fists and pounded them into the supports between the screens. The crack of the wood shocked him out of his tirade. The outside hanging shutters bounced against the house. Soon his anger morphed into confusion. He wanted some real answers about how he came to be black with two white parents.

The sounds from the back porch must have drawn the attention of Charlie's grandfather. The squeak from the kitchen door made the young man jump.

"Hey, there you are. We've been wondering about you. Went for a morning walk?" His grandfather's voice didn't waver as the old man studied the damage. "Looks like you have some repair work to do before you go home. You can get a new brace and the tools out of the shed after breakfast."

"I walked to the old boarding house. The owner would only let me through the back door to the kitchen. They have a black cook. He'd heard gossip Grandpa. People say I'm not a real Bueller." His fist balled up ready to hit something or someone.

The old man held his hand up to stop Charlie as he checked the door to the kitchen. "I don't think we need to upset everyone with this.

They are so busy clattering dishes and pans I don't think they will notice. Now, what is it you're talking about? Who said you're not a Bueller."

"I can't say I haven't suspected, but I didn't dare let my mind go there for ma's sake. Now I have to know. We buried the man I have called Pa for twenty years. Who am I Grandpa? Was Ma...raped?" He gagged, and then bent over like he was sick.

"You okay boy?"

"No, but I'm not going to be sick right now." The young man pulled out his handkerchief and wiped his mouth anyway. "I want to cool off a bit before coming in if you don't mind."

"You do that," Charlie could tell his grandfather was clenching his jaw. "You better remember, that was my son we buried yesterday as well. I know you have questions, and I have some stuff I want to go over with you. I sure as hell didn't think it would all come out this way. Get yourself under control and we are going to my den."

"I'm sorry Grandpa. I didn't mean any disrespect about Pa, or nothing."

"I ain't mad at you son."

Charlie watched his grandfather's shoulders slump. "Mind if I wait with you?"

"No Grandpa, I don't mind at all." I'd hug you, old man, if I thought you'd let me. I could sure use one.

17

After a time the two men's steps were sharp and fast as they made their way through the house.

"There you are. Where are you going?

"To my den, don't worry about it."

"But, breakfast is ready. It will get cold?" Lula's voice followed.

"We'll be fine."

On entering the den, the old man motioned for his grandson to sit in a huge leather chair in front of a big walnut desk. The older man opened a locked drawer and then reached across to the desk laying the Family Bible under Charlie's nose. He laid an envelope in front of his grandson containing a statement from the doctor who delivered the first baby of Henry and Lula Bueller. On it, he recorded the birth of a white baby. The huge Bible recorded a male infant born to Henry and Lula Bueller Dec. 1 1885. The infant's given name was Charles Xavier Bueller.

"If you like, we can look at the birth records at the Methodist Church later. I only need to call the minister. However, I want you to see something first. Turn back about three pages of that Bible."

"Grandpa, please!" Charlie cried out. He held his head in his hands as if trying to recover from a blow. "What...What happened to the white baby boy?"

"You grew up healthy and strong."

"Me?"

"Son, your skin is a light shade of brown. Yes, you have course, wiry hair, but your skin didn't turn until you were nearly a year old. Oh, we noticed it was growing darker, and the doc thought maybe you had the jaundice or something, but the baby was you."

Charlie slowly picked up the corner of a page. There he saw the record of his parent's marriage almost ten months before his birth.

Another page flipped slowly over and another. His mouth dropped as he looked at the script on the page.

"Read it out loud. I want you to hear it from your own mouth."

"Walter Bueller, a slave owner from Alabama, did bed and impregnate slave Bessie who conceived a child. A male child was born with white skin to Bessie. The child remained white. Walter and wife Helena adopted the boy. This record is to be sealed in wax by Walter Bueller until such time as descendant breaks such seal. The letter is signed by Walter Bueller and witnessed by Lon Argo Attorney at law 20 March, 1791."

"I'm colored because of a man who raped a black slave! How disgusting is that?"

"Yes, and not because of anything your mother did. She knew about this and chose my Henry anyway. She is a jewel your ma is." Grandpa Bueller's voice cracked and he slouched in his chair.

"Charlie, that happened three generations before I was born. As much as I don't like that part of our family tree, it was common practice for slave owners to copulate with female slaves to increase slave populations."

John Bueller rose from his chair and walked to Charlie. Taking the young man's shoulders, he positioned himself in front of Charlie gaze. Voice steady he spoke, "Look me in the eye's son."

When the young man complied, the elder Bueller smiled. "That is how you hold your head when you are out on that street. You keep your nose parallel to the ground and your shoulders straight. You have nothing to hide."

"There is a mirror on that wall." John walked to the large mirror. "Look, compare the set of your jaw to mine. It's the same kind of strong Greek jaw line, the nose the same straight Greek nose. My son," The older Bueller swallowed so hard it was audible. "My son had those same features."

Charlie threw his arms around his grandfather. "Thank you Grandpa. I won't doubt again." The grandfather gave the boy in the man a pat on the back and pulled away from the hug.

"Good, let's get some sausage and biscuits, I'm starving."

Charlie cleared his throat and stood straight. "That sounds great."

The two men entered the kitchen with an air of comradeship between them. Charlie knew their relationship had grown that morning.

"It's about time the two of you showed up." Lula looked at her son. "What's going on?"

"I learned some things. I'll talk to you about it later." He tilted his head toward the children.

Lula nodded.

"Vernie, Jack, take the children upstairs and dress them for travel. We'll be heading home today and I'd like to catch an early enough train for us to get back before dark."

Spicy sausage in white gravy slid around Charles tongue as he chewed Grandmother's sweet southern style biscuits. Every bite was like a revelation in a new life, bursting with truth in its flavor. His third plateful neatly polished clean, the heaviness of the biscuits swelling filled his stomach to a pleasurable discomfort.

"Goodness, I don't think I've ever seen you eat like that son." Lula Bueller commented from a voice hoarse with a chuckle behind the words.

"I know M ." A huge belch rang out before he finished the word Ma.

"Was that a compliment I heard?" Grandma Bueller chimed in. The room exploded with laughter.

Charlie broke away looking into his mother's eyes, "George," His face grew pale. "if he marries that girl without knowing, they could be in for a surprise of their own."

"He knows," Grandfather chimed in. "I told George last night. He cursed us and said he would never claim us as his family. I doubt we'll hear much from him."

"That explains a lot. He changed toward me like we quit being brothers. He called me nigger before he left last night. It was when nobody was around. That girl's family is putting him through academy and may help him into politics he said."

"I had a feeling that girl had something to do with his nose in the air."

"Ma, it's not at you. I think he'll talk to you."

"No, I won't have it. I have one less son."

"Ma!"

A matronly hand slapped the air dismissing any argument as Lula Bueller turned away.

Chapter 3 Changes

Charlie sat on the edge of his chair, elbows on the table and head in hands. His youngest siblings were asking questions he didn't know how to answer: "Is daddy coming back from heaven? Didn't daddy love us and want to stay? Why are you a nigger?" The answers seemed obvious until the questions were asked.

He felt hot anger toward the funeral director in Blue Rivers. He'd never thought of himself as a 'nigger'. Who ever invented the damn word? How could he come to terms with the heritage all his family shared, but only he bore? What would he do with his life? Would the boarding house be the only place he could belong? What about work and a life of his own. Maybe being the oldest son of Henry and Lula Bueller would be the only real place for him in the world. Would that be enough?

He forced his mind to more practical questions. What about money lost from pa's job? A feeling of dread ran through his veins, heart pumping so fast it felt like it would jump out of his chest. Charlie rushed from the kitchen, out the back door to the porch where he dipped his head over the side railing and let go of the bacon and eggs they ate at breakfast. Thank goodness nobody saw him. The others were all visiting at Dr. and Mrs. Wilson's home. The Wilsons were neighbors across the street and the first to welcome them to Wyman many years back. Charlie remembered Doc bringing half a dozen men to help erect the walls of the huge house.

Sweeping the depot floors wouldn't pay much. With a large family and only two boarders, money would be tight. Ma kept up with the open lunch tables and people brought food to help fill the pots. Enough remained to provide most of the family and boarders with other meals. Nobody who wanted a free lunch dared make any slur against one of her children. The picture of twelve diners at a time around the huge table built by pa, himself, and George made Charlie feel warmer and his stomach settled. Many times he'd seen a guest chewing on a piece of roast beef while listening to the person to their right talk about their morning, then once the chewer swallowed they'd answer with their own day's plan. To some it may seem dull, but the excitement of community in the room charged the whole house with energy.

He walked through the back door into the laundry and back to the normally warm and inviting kitchen. He pumped water over his hands and splashed his face.

"Hey, that's a smile I've missed. What's in that head of yours brother? "

"Oh, hey Fred, I didn't realize I was smiling."

"Is that a bad thing Charlie? Come back to us brother."

"Oh, I'm here." He dried his face. "I figured you'd be off beating up someone for money. Why aren't you out teaching someone a lesson?"

"Well if you mean why I don't have a fight or a boxing class it's because I have a night off. I decided to take a night and let my bruises heal."

"Ah ha, somebody landed one did they?"

"Happens"

"Not to ma."

"What?"

"Don't tell her I said anything, but you remember when we disappeared after pa's funeral?"

"Yeah, kind of, there was a lot going on."

"We went back to the funeral home, and ma took down that mortician."

"No, you're kidding. Tell me the whole story."

The two young men went to the barn so nobody could hear. Charlie told his brother the whole story with all the action and exaggeration he could muster.

"We found him in the basement embalming a body. When he turned to tell us to get out, ma placed an uppercut in his bread basket. He fell to his knees and ma told me to push the body from the table right over on top of him." Charlie couldn't help but laugh with his brother.

"Wow! Ma really asked you to do that and you really pushed a dead man on top of him? Oh, this is one for the books my brother."

"Shh, Ma doesn't want anyone to know. I guess pa must have

taught her just like he did us."

"I'll say, ma never seemed to have a lot of fear but, oh brother!" Nothing could make Fred stop laughing until he grabbed his belly and bent over. Slowly he hiccupped through the end of the spasm of merriment, but his smile seemed a permanent feature.

Charlie had joined the contagious laughter. The dark gloom left and Charlie felt he could be honest for the first time since returning to Wyman. "Yeah, after ma punched him so hard he fell over! I have to say, it made me feel like a twelve year old on his mommy's skirts. I guess I felt that way most of the day."

"You did right to hang back. Can you imagine what would have happened if you had taken it into your own hands. They would have thrown you in jail. Would that make ma happy?"

"I suppose not."

His laughter turned to a groaning anguish. "I miss pa. I wish something could take away the pictures of that day he died. I tried to hold him together, but I couldn't do it." Tears were starting at the corners of his eyes. Wiping them away as if they were intruders, he tried to turn away from Fred."

"I don't know what exactly happened that day, but I do know Mrs. Wilson said nothing could have saved him." Fred put an arm around Charlie's shoulder. "I miss him too and I do miss George even with his nose in the air. He always had such high ambitions, but he sure shocked us when he left the way he did. It's like he didn't even care that ma was hurting."

'Since his eighteenth birthday, he'd been treating me more and more like some disease. I remember Pa told George if he ever caught him calling me nigger again, he'd throttle him. Within less than a year we went from brothers to enemies all because of that little bitch and her family. I wish I knew why he had to take it so far. Why can't he at least talk to us?" Charles felt the anger chilling his heart.

"He made his decision Charlie. Ma made her decision too. But, I think I'm going to go have a chat with him when he gets back from lawyer school."

"When is that?"

"One of my friends talks to him and keeps him up to date. He keeps me up on what's going on with George too. I think he only did it for his girl's family. Have to admit, they are giving him a free ride."

"Get him to meet us somewhere; I want to talk to him. He needs to at least tell ma he's sorry."

Fred looked at his oldest brother. "Agree with you there, but don't hold your breath that she'll even give him the chance. Charlie, if just talking about George makes you clench up like that with your fists, hell your whole body, what happens when you see him? I don't think you should see him."

Charlie didn't say any more about George. He pulled out his pocket watch. "I'd better get down to the railroad office. I have to sweep up after the morning train and set out new linens in the water closet. There is talk of redoing the depot to make it fancy. The railroad is fixing to have this be almost as upscale a hub as they have in Chicago. Go figure, little Wyman, but that hotel down there is awfully fancy and lots of people like to come here just for that experience. It's funny isn't it, people come to a town just to stay at a hotel a day or two. It must be something."

Charlie waved as he strode down the street toward the Railroad Depot.

"Charlie, put up the broom and come here." The railroad superintendent called to him as he swept the last bit of dirt out the door.

"Yes sir? I kind of wanted to talk to you too."

The railroad man just held his hand up.

"I gotta let ya go. Too many people are uncomfortable since the accident and nobody much cares to have a nigra around. To tell ya the truth, you make me and the crew damned uncomfortable since that day. No hard feelings son." He held out some coins.

"Sir, I need this job and nobody had a problem before."

"Sorry, you have to go. Take your pay and go home. Don't make a scene now."

"I guess I have to, don't say there's no bad feelings. I feel pretty damn bad about it and to tell the truth, you owe a lot more to my pa, and me than these few coins. That's a debt no money can pay."

Dejected, Charles took the coins. He counted up fifty cents. "What's the railroad going to do for my family? Pa died working here, his body torn to shreds by one of your trains." He could hear the agitation in his own voice. His fist curled around the coins until he felt them bite his flesh.

"Cool down there Charlie, I sent a check for fifty dollars to your ma. That makes the end of it."

"You son of a bitch, you don't care at all that my pa died helping this railroad. He was the best porter you ever had. Every passenger loved him and so did the crews."

"Hey if not for him, you would never have worked here. Be grateful now and go home."

There was nothing left to say. Charlie felt like someone rubbed coal all over him from head to toe. As much as he wanted to hurt the devil behind the desk, making an enemy of the railroad wouldn't help at all. How could he tell his mother he'd lost what little money he did bring in. He raised his head up and noticed he was standing in front of the saloon. "Hmm, one thing I do pretty well."

By the time he got home that night, he'd turned fifty cents into two dollars. It was a start. His future seemed to be in gambling; the one profession that didn't much care about color, as long as there was money on the table. Henry taught his sons the dos and don'ts of poker Texas hold em, five card stud and draw and even bridge. He knew how to spot a cheat, an amateur, and a tell.

He handed the money to his mother. "I'm afraid that's the end of my job ma. The superintendent let me go. He said I made people nervous."

She patted his hand with her own pasty palm and laughed when he tried brushing the stickiness off. "You'll have to wash it off. It's biscuit dough."

"Ma, did you hear. I'm out of a job. He did say he's sending you a fifty dollar settlement."

"Son, I heard and I'm sort of relieved. I could sure use you around here. Your father took care of the books, and all the business transactions. I just don't have the time for all that. With the settlement we'll get by for a while."

It seemed like a lot of money, but he never knew how fast money could go. Charlie had a talent for numbers and accounts. Vernie helped what she could at fourteen. She spent much of her time taking care of the two youngest siblings. Charles talked to his sister about running a schedule. The youngest children would be fed lunch immediately after morning play time then put down for a nap with a story.

Lula was having trouble finding time to teach Roy and Earl so she asked Vernie to try to fit their vocabulary and sums into her day. Roy of course needed more time and advanced lessons than Earl, but the six year old learned how to add his one, two and three pluses and spell simple words like cat, hat, and fat by the time he was seven. Roy's lessons included multiplication, division, reading and writing and simple chores such as planting vegetables.

Things seemed to be fairly smooth until one day Charlie saw his mother standing in the middle of the dining room just staring. "Ma, are you okay?"

"Yes son, I'm just tired and this mess is kind of overwhelming me at the moment."

"You don't have to do these free meals ma. Why don't you stop? I can put up a sign saying there will be no more town lunches if you like."

"Charlie, I don't think you realize how important these meals are." She motioned to a chair as she sat. "Honey, this meal brings in more food to feed this family than I could ever grow or buy. It's how this family eats. It's also brought good will and fellowship to the town. The mayor to the poorest has sat here together chatting away. That can't be bought and the town helps support us as long as I keep that open.

"I don't understand how feeding so many brings in more food." Bewildered, he sat resting his chin in his hands, elbows on the table.

"Charlie, quit doing that. Its not good for you posture. How many times have I told you?"

He sat straight in the chair looking at her still obedient to her motherly commands.

"Maybe you've never noticed all the food the diners bring in. Just about everything we eat at other meals comes in that front door from meat to milk and more vegetables that I can ever grow in my garden."

"I've noticed some of them bring stuff, but I figured that mostly took care of the noon meals."

"It does take care of the noon meals, but … Oh, let me show you." She motioned for him to follow her to the kitchen. "Look in that icebox."

Charlie opened the door of the cooler and it almost overflowed with cheeses, milk, chunks of meat all wrapped up and marked. His eyes grew wide as he followed her into her private pantry filled with flour, sugar, potatoes, onions, and other vegetables and dry goods he'd never seen. "Ma, you've been keeping all this hidden from us."

"I wouldn't exactly call it hidden, I just never drew attention to it. I'm afraid if the townspeople found out how much I've got stocked up, they'd quit bringing things. This doesn't even count the smoke house out back or the corn I haven't had ground into meal yet. I have to keep using it up before it gets buggy." She had a broad smile on her face as if she'd shared the secret of life itself.

"Wow, okay we keep the noon meals open and you keep making bread and whatever else to keep this under control." He felt dumfounded as if he'd just learned the secret to life. He shook his head. "Okay, I guess you need more help with cleaning up after the lunches then."

"That would be good."

"Okay, I'll talk to Vernie."

"Tread carefully there. She's not in the greatest of moods. Verie does a lot around here already."

Charlie ignored most of what she'd said. *Ma, you need help and I'm getting you help. Venie will be just fine.* He found his sister in the room she shared with Pearl at the back end of the first floor.

"Vernie, I hate to ask more of you." The look of 'are you kidding me' in Vernie's eye made him flinch. She was definitely her mother's daughter. Backing off two steps, he ventured into the danger zone. "Ma's having trouble getting the house chores all done what with taking care of all the laundry and cooking. I hate to ask more of you, but ma could use help with scrubbing floors."

"Charlie, I'm so busy the only time I get to do my own stuff is when those kids are napping. I can't. I'm already taking care of them all day, including their schooling. Why can't Jack do some scrubbing? Doesn't that new ringer washer help ma with laundry?"

Charlie backed away like he might be attacked. "I'm sorry sis, I didn't. I just thought maybe after the lunch crowd. What's wrong with you?" *Women, I've about had it with this moodiness. Vernie can just grow up.*

She threw her arms in the air and then slapped them against her thighs. "So what about Jack and why does she need so much extra help with that new wringer washer? I didn't just suddenly turn into ma when pa died."

"All right, calm down. I didn't think of Jack, and you are twins. I keep forgetting he's old enough to take more chores on. What does he do anyway?"

"Mostly he plays ball with his friends up at the park."

Maybe I should back off on her, and she does do quite a bit. It probably wouldn't hurt to give her a compliment. "Okay, I'll talk to him and ma will back me up. There's nothing wrong with him learning to scrub floors." He backed up a bit. "Vernie, I don't say it enough, but thank you for all your help. It's been hard since pa died. I guess he helped more around the house than we knew."

"Yeah; sure, He mostly kept us busy so ma could get her work done. I loved Pa too, but he wasn't an angel." She threw herself on the bed crying."

He lost his composure and yelled at his sister. "What the Sam Hill is wrong with you?"

"I'm invisible till somebody want's something?"

" I'll admit we have taken you for granted lately. I'll get Jack to do the scrubbing. I keep forgetting he's the same age as you. You're the oldest girl and Jack is in the middle of us boys, and there's a bunch of us. I'm sorry, I didn't pay more attention."

He heard something, probably her pillow, hit her side of the door. Wiping his hand across his forehead he flicked his frustration into the wind.

Charlie found Lula in the laundry room with huge piles of laundry all around her and a woven basket full of wet cloths. "Ma, I think something is wrong with Vernie. She just tore into me like a cat. Usually she's so quiet."

"Well son, your sister is fourteen. She's become a woman, if you know what I mean by that."

His face screwed up as he tried to solve the riddle. Then his eyes became wide enough for the whites to almost pop out of his face. "Oh Jeez, yes, I do know what you mean Pa made sure we understood how women work that way. My Lord ma," he strode toward the back door with the basket of wet clothing."

He heard his mother laughing as he hurried out the back door.

Lula showed Jack how to scrub the floors without leaving streaks, and even let him wash some clothes in the new wringer washer. The washer became an essential part of their daily routine. Other items of import were purchased to help the house run more smoothly such as a treadle sewing machine. Even Vernie fell in love with making curtains and a new dress on the miracle machine. His mother insisted on a piano so she could teach lessons, starting with her own children. It wasn't long before she had two more students. Charlie and the rest of the family learned of a talent she'd hidden through their childhood.

Five dollars went to repair the buckboard which had rotted boards from its old days of carrying them through wet weather. Now, they had a homemade box shaped wagon that left little room for the older wagon in the barn, so weather had broken it down even more. He repaired the wheels, wagon floor, and seat. Fred and Jack helped Charles cut the trees and take them to the mill.

The new washer, piano, sewing machine and repairs to the house whittled the settlement down quickly. Charlie hadn't worked for nearly three months. October rushed by and winter came early. By that time there was little cash in hand. Charlie talked to his mother, who seemed too busy to pay a lot of attention.

"Ma, please I need help here. I'm doing these books and we are out of money. We've got to do something!"

"I heard you son. Let's sit down at the table and see where we're at."

Mother and son sat at the table with their heads together for a half hour before any interruption. Vernie flounced in with Earl and Pearl just up from their naps. "Hi mommy," Earl yawned. "It's time for a snack."

"Okay babies, how about milk and jelly bread?"

"Yay," the youngest Buellers cheered in unison, suddenly very awake. Lula laughed and helped Vernie get them in their seats.

"Charlie, I think you know what to do and how best to arrange things. I certainly don't get the time to figure that stuff out."

How do women change from one thing to the next without a thought of finishing the first? How did pa do this?

Over the next two days, Charlie used any minute he found to figure out how to make the boarding house profitable. In one of those moments of ingenuity, he saw the answers clearly. He wrote his notes on some tablet paper and waited for a chance to present it to his mother.

"I never would have thought of this."

"Is it okay? I mean it moves the family into two big rooms. Do you mind sleeping in the same room as Vernie and Pearl?"

"Son, you have no idea how much that will help clear up my loneliness." She turned quickly away and he knew she was fighting tears. "Let's present it tomorrow to the kids so they all know what's going on. Maybe we can get through it during the little ones' nap."

The next afternoon Charlie called them all to the kitchen table. The worn table top bore the indents of hands rubbing back and forth to clean the spills that would stain its surface otherwise. Initials were carved too deep for sanding and waxed over to a high shine. These things bore memories of days gone and hopes for more to come. He'd looked at pa's chair, empty for nearly a year and waited. All family members filed into the benches on each side. He smiled at the memory of pa, himself and George building the table and the long benches that were much easier than chairs. However, special care went into making two chairs for each end for the mother and father of the growing family. Now he watched as the members slid into their places. *Thank goodness, Earl and Pearl are sleeping.*

"Ma, do you know what this is about?" Jack asked.

"I'm afraid so son. Charles has been keeping the books. It seems we've gone through most of the money from the railroad settlement."

"I can take on a few more fights." Fred eagerly offered. "In fact a guy in Omaha asked to manage me on a professional circuit. I'd love to do it and be one less big mouth to feed."

"If you do that son, it's of your own accord. Don't ask me to make that sacrifice."

"Mother, it's not a sacrifice. It's an honor and challenge. I can also teach boxing when I come here in the off season."

"There's an off season for boxing?" Charlie asked surprised.

"At my level there can be. I'm just getting in and won't have as many fights as the seasoned pros."

"Listen to him ma; Fred the fighter! He's making good use of the years punching the feed sack full of straw." Jack's excitement boiled over. "How about that?"

"Pa taught us a lot too, didn't he Charlie?" Fred quickly added. "He made sure we had the tools to defend ourselves. He liked teaching us boxing for sport too. Remember guys?" Nods confirmed as he pushed his point. "See Jack and Charlie both agree"

"Yup, and I think ma watched from a corner somewhere." Merry laughter filled the kitchen, but Lula glared at her son over the secret he was supposed to keep.

"I didn't know ma ever punched the bag."

She cleared her throat. "That's about enough of teasing your old ma. So I got a few punches in on the bag when you boys were growing up. Your pa wanted me to hold my own; now, back to the matter in front of us."

"Which one?"

"Fred!" Everybody settled down. They saw that spark lighting in her eyes, that warning of fire to come. "Son, you are only sixteen years old. I don't like you going off like that. You're too young."

"I'll be seventeen in a couple of weeks and the first year is all training and small bouts. I'll probably start as a sparring partner."

"What's that?"

"That's the guy the professional fighters practice with."

She let out a big sigh and looked around the table for support. Charles noticed her eyes moved toward the ceiling. "I guess your father would consent. Promise me no major fights until you're at least eighteen."

"I promise." Jack stood up and kissed his mother's cheek."

"That is not necessary. " She blushed as the table erupted in giggles.

Charles, sitting in the chair once occupied by his father spoke up "Okay, can we get back to keeping this family from going broke?"

Twelve year old Roy took offense. "You're not Daddy, why are you acting like you are."

"I'm not trying to act like Daddy, Roy. I'm the oldest and I guess I presumed ma and pa would want me to take some charge around here. Not from ma, but just help out.

"Roy," Lula soothed, "Charlie has to help out with the running of the boarding house and the money. I have too much to do. It's what daddy wanted. He wrote it down that if anything ever happened to him, I should ask Charlie to take over some of the duties. He's not taking over as your daddy. I'm still your mama and I'll take care of you. Okay."

"Okay, but I'm twelve. I'm not a baby and I can help too. Daddy would want that. I know he would."

"Would you like ma to assign you some responsibilities. You've done most of your schooling so I think that's something important."

"Okay. Sorry I acted like a baby."

Jack spoke up: "I'm fourteen and I miss daddy too. I want to act like a baby sometimes."

"Really?"

"Yes, me too Roy," Vernie said.

"We all miss pa, my children. Maybe we should take a break before we talk anymore about this."

"I'm not sure we'd get everyone back around the table. The little ones will be waking up soon."

"Okay, take a minute to at least remember your pa before we go forward. You think I don't miss him Charlie." Lula's voice broke as she pointed her finger at him. "I'm sorry kids, I need some coffee. Does anyone else want something to drink?" She brought herself up short and cleared her throat.

Charlie didn't answer. He couldn't, all he seemed capable of at the moment was feeling confused.

Lula served coffee and milk around. Then the door creaked and they all looked around to see two cherubs standing hand in hand.

"Oh boy, now what?"

"Charlie, shut up. They can be here too." Vernie scolded.

"Why am I everyone's villain here?" He stood up and snorted as he stomped through the kitchen and out the back door.

The white barn loomed over his dark cloud. He battled the punching bag until it started to drop straw from opened seams.

"Looks like we need a new one brother"

"Damn Fred you spooked me." He breathed heavily, bent over with his hands on his knees. "Sorry – I had – to get – it out."

"I know, but nobody is thinking of you as a villain. You think you have to do it all, and you don't. We all still have bruised souls from Pa dying."

"Yes, but none of you were there when he died. All of his blood spilled under that train. I couldn't hold him together." For the first time since his father's death, Charles allowed himself to give in to his pain. He didn't care what anybody thought. The images rerunning in his mind, gave him a pain in his chest. Each intake of breath felt like someone was stabbing him in the heart."

"I can't even imagine how bad that was for you. I just can't understand why it happened." Both men let out their grief. Charlie's anger began to melt and he felt a warmth flow through his body he hadn't felt since that day.

"My dear brother," Fred sobbed, "you have never been a villain in this family. The fact is we are a family and sometimes we rub each other the wrong way. Everyone is still missing pa. You know that. I'd love to see you smile again. I don't give a damn what other people say and neither does anyone else in that house. We love you brother." Charles looked at Fred who hadn't spoken that many words together that he could remember, and he never talked about love and such."

Charlie's pains subsided to his relief.

"Wow, I never knew my sixteen," Charles held up his hand, "soon to be seventeen, year old brother could talk so much. I know I never gave you credit for being so wise."

"Get outta here. If you tell anyone that I got sappy, I'll kick your butt. You may be older, but I'm just as big and I know a thing or two about boxing."

"Oh, now is that a challenge?" The two walked back to the house play punching each other's arms. Charles smiled. Later he realized he'd given Fred exactly what he needed as well as Fred giving him reassurance. The brothers walked through the back door to the kitchen.

"I'm sorry ma." Charlie pulled his chair up to the table. "I guess I just needed some time."

"Son, I understand, but I think you need to talk to Earl and Pearl. They don't understand what's going on at all."

"You didn't do that?"

"Charlie, it needs to come from you. I told them you were feeling bad, but they don't understand why. Honey, you've never ever been the villain. We had issues we hadn't discussed as a family. We all reacted."

"Overreacted you mean?"

"No, Charlie I don't think it was so much overreaction, it was time to get stuff out. It's okay we all need to know that every one of us hurts inside since Henry died, including me." Her deep intake of breath was followed by a slow release of air. Her shoulders relaxed noticeably. She smiled. "Go talk to your baby sister and brother."

"What about the family talk?"

"Would you mind if I read that at supper Charlie?" Fred offered. "If they see you, me and ma all united, it may go over better."

Charles stared at his brother as if he saw him for the first time. "My brother is a man. I'd be happy for you to take that off my shoulders Fred."

A new look of respect passed from bother to brother. Lula sat smiling.

The family and boarders sat around the long, formal, dining table for supper. Lula decided their three current boarders should take part in the conversation about changes.

"My son's Fred and Charles have formed a plan to help finances at The Bueller Boarding House. You should all hear the proposal. Fred, before Vernie and I serve the meal, would you open the discussion with the plan?"

"Certainly mother," he looked around the table. Charlie was surprised at Fred's ability to speak so eloquently to a group."

"To tell you the truth, my big brother here drew up most of the proposal, but ma and I have reviewed it and feel it's a good one. Now we would like the input of all here." He paused and looked up at the group. He looked to Charlie who nodded.

"This is the proposal, and then we can open for discussion during our meal. First we should sell the buckboard. Charlie rebuilt it and some farmer will scoop it up for haying and such. We think ten dollars is a good price. Second, if I leave to start training for the boxing circuit that will free up some room. We could move Charlie in with Jack, Roy and Earl." He held up his hand as Jack groaned. Third, Ma moves a bed in with Vernie and Pearl. That opens up two good sized rooms. Finally, we open those rooms for more boarders. That's the plan we worked out. Why don't you all think about it and we'll let ma and Vernie serve supper."

Charlie clapped he was so impressed by his brother. Then he heard clapping fill the room.

Vernie pushed a trolley of rib steaks cooked in onions, mashed potatoes, gravy, fresh garden peas and two baskets of fresh baked biscuits. A universal "awe" filled the room.

"I've smelled that food and I'm hungry as all get out." Mrs. Black's mouth almost visibly watered.

"Me too, Ma you've this is a feast." Charlie added.

Nobody seemed interested in discussing the changes. Charlie looked at his mother who winked back. "Well done ma, well done." Nothing sells a good idea like a steak dinner.

The next day the changes began for Charlie as his plan to rearrange the rooms, created more changes than he'd anticipated. Nobody had any idea how much trouble a good idea could cause.

Chapter 4: Boarding House Shuffle

Charlie never dreamed switching people around a house took so many steps. Fred made the announcement, but left the very next day. Jack had finished most of his schooling except Bible lessons and piano. After his conversation, if he could call it that, with Vernie; Charlie decided it was time Jack took on more responsibility. With all the work needed to rearrange sleeping quarters and Fred gone, the opportunity became a necessity.

"Ma, Charlie says I have to help him build beds. Can you tell him I don't have to? I want to go play ball with my friend and the park.

A two acre park only a few blocks from the boarding house had put in a new ball park. Teams were formed almost daily. Nearly every boy in town wanted a spot on a team and Jack was no different.

"Well, I kind of told Charlie that if he needs you, I'd tell you to help. So, since I already told Charlie I guess you'll have to play ball later. Charlie, do you think you could give him some time off once in a while for baseball?"

"Deal, but now I want you to go with me to Evans Lumber.

"Ah,"

"Jackie, you know better than to argue with me. Besides building is a great way to practice measuring and learn carpentry."

Jack stormed out in front of Charlie who whispered, "Thanks ma," on his way out.

"You can go with me to the new lumber store. I think they may have some patterns for me too. When we're done there you can go to the ball park."

"You use patterns? I just thought ma used those to sew."

"Well, you've learned something already. Patterns are used for lots of things. Some call them diagrams, or blueprints, or schematics. I prefer the step by step pattern in their how to patterns."

"Oh," Jack looked blank.

Charles smiled. "You'll see when we get there. We get to take the buckboard."

"Really, can I sit in the back?"

"Yup "

Hitching their one remaining horse Trotter to the harness was more of a production than Charlie remembered. Once the animal was secured he could see Jack rolling his eyes. "Oh, you think you could do better?"

"No, I've never done it. You've done it lots of times. Did you forget how?" The boy's sarcasm made the older brother smile.

"Are you related to Vernie somehow?"

"Well umm, she's my twin what do you think?"

"Well boy, it's time you learned a thing or two. What are you twelve? I was building our house at twelve."

"I'm not a boy and I'm fourteen."

"I'll bet they heard that at the house. Now that we all know you're a young man, we can expect you to act like one. It's time to grow up there Jackie boy." Charles continued to tease Jack knowing the more the boy protested, the more Jack would be obligated to prove himself a grownup.

"Stop that, I can do a lot of things, but you always asked Fred to help you."

"I have been neglecting you."

"Whatever that means"

"Woops, back to school for you."

"No, just tell me what it means."

"It means, I haven't paid attention to you."

"That's right, Charlie, you have neglected me, and Roy."

"Well then today we start your training as a man. Maybe Roy can join us later."

The new lumber store looked bright and clean. The Evans brothers built it to sell lumber from their father's mill and kept it stocked with tools and hardware as well. The new brick building looked plain compared to the fancier stores on Main Street with all the storefronts topped with staggered brick making patterns, or arches and painted signs. What good was fancy for lumber stores? Yet, they designed a spectacular, carved, wooden sign with carvings so intricate, any wood crafter would envy it. They'd even carved items people might build like a house, barn, tables and chairs, and in the last corner a cradle. In the middle of it all was their name Evans Lumber.

A bell over the door jingled as they entered.

"Hey Charlie, is that your brother Jackie?" Both of the new customers nodded. "Welcome to our new store."

"Please call me Jack. I'm grown up."

"Jack, be polite."

"He did say please. It was my mistake Jack." Bill held a hand out to Jack who shook it shooting Charlie a look that said "ah, ha."

"You did a fine job here Bill. You and Jerry should be very happy with this place. Who is your wood carver?"

It's one of Jerry's hidden talents. He's been working on carving since he was able to hold the tools.

"I'll have to keep that in mind."

"Don't have any complaints yet. Did you come for the opening or can I get you something?"

"Well let's call it both. I smell some coffee." He sniffed the air dragging in the smell of new milled lumber, new building odors; coffee, and more smells than he could name. "Do you have any patterns for bunks or cots?"

"Sure, are you expanding?"

"Not the house, but the number of boarders yes. We've got some extra space now Fred's moved out and we're going to pile the boys in one room and the girls in another."

"Well, let's get you started." Bill pointed Charlie and Jack to a table and served them coffee. "I'll get you those patterns.. Jerry is out back helping a customer. It's some new guy staying at the hotel until he finds someplace to stay. I can sure point him your direction."

"I appreciate that Bill. Do you mind if I put a sign on the window to sell our buckboard?"

"Well, how much do you want?"

"I fixed it all up so it looks almost new. We're asking ten."

"I think I'll just buy that from you then. We have a need for a delivery wagon. Have you heard of all the people moving into town and building houses? It's a boon for sure."

"I've been pretty busy. I had noticed a couple being framed across the street."

Bill left Charlie and Jack to look over their patterns.

"What do you think Jack?" Charlie could see Jack was intent on the patterns and felt a surge of pride in his brother, though he didn't think he could take much credit for it."

"We don't need those fancy, girly ones. I like the look of the cots, but I think we should make some of these." Jack picked out a pattern for simple bunks. The frame left room under the bed for storage of boots and other items. "Slats could be made of a slightly flexible wood, each long enough to prevent falling from the sides of the frame."

"That's just the ticket. That looks simple and durable. Should we make them out of oak do you suppose?"

"Good choice on the pattern, but oak needs a good saw and I'd use pegs instead of nails."

Charlie looked up into the pink face of a man about his own age. "You know something about carpentry?"

"Sure do, my name is Carl Travers." He put a hand out.

Charlie stood up, hesitated a moment and then confidently shook hands with Carl. His brown skinned fingers wrapped around the warm palm of a new friend. Charlie knew his shock showed in his wide eyes.

"Lordamercy man, did I scare ya or something."

"A little, where are you from?"

"Up north in the Dakotas, South Dakota actually, we still tend to think of it as all one territory, except the politicians." His broad smile made Charlie forget the differences.

"Hey!"

"Oh, I'm sorry Jack." He looked at Carl. "This is my brother Jack. He's helping me and learning how to build beds."

"Yeah Mr., I picked the pattern, see?"

"Call me Carl and Jack that's a great choice for a bed."

"We gotta build a bunch of beds." Jack responded the teenage squeal of his voice.

"Hey, that sounds like the sound I made when I became a man."

Carl's ability to connect with people wasn't lost on Charlie. He liked the man and hoped Carl would be staying around. It would be nice to have a friend that wasn't family. He'd never had that sort of friendship before.

"Have you heard of the Bueller Boarding House?"

"Can't say as I have, I just arrived on the train and I'm hoping to drum up some work."

"Our mother is the owner. I help her out quite a bit. We're expanding by combining the family into fewer rooms and opening up more for boarders. Would you be interested in a room?

Charlie had determined the man was exactly the kind of boarder that would appeal to his mother and fit in well with the other boarders.

"To tell you the truth, I'm more of a bunk house kind of a guy. I'm not used to having a lot of people around. If you have a barn with a loft, I'd be a willing renter and helper."

"Well, if we can get ma to agree to it, I think we could make accommodations in the barn loft. We do have one horse in there though if you don't mind the smell."

Carl didn't seem to flinch at the idea of animal smells. "If you can take a bit off the rent, I clean the stall daily and promise not to bring the smells in the house. In the winter I'll be quite cozy with a couple of quilts and straw mattress for bedding. I'm going to be drumming up work as a carpenter and that would suit me fine until I get set up with work."

Charles wondered if the man was too good to be true. Why was he so friendly to him with his dark skin? Most unfamiliar people seemed to take offense at his very presence. Carl didn't ask any questions about his family and no comments about Jack being a white brother. What's the guy's game? Is he really as down to earth as he seems. That handshake told Charlie he could trust Carl, but he wasn't ready to leap to a decision though he badly wanted the man's friendship.

"I hope your ma don't mind that I do like to go to the saloon and have a couple games of poker and a shot or two of whiskey."

"As long as you don't come in drunk and wake everybody up, or burn down the house we'll do fine."

Jack sat patiently waiting for the men to acknowledge him. "Do you want to help us make the beds? We can take the cot pattern too so you can have a cot to sleep on. Straw mattresses are prickly."

"I'd appreciate that Jack. You're a decision maker, I can tell."

"Thank you. He treats me like a little boy." Jack pointed at Charlie.

"Sorry buddy, I'll try to do better."

Charlie scowled at Carl. "Thanks a whole heck of a lot."

"Oh you're welcome." Carl seemed unapologetic. "Lordamercy man, I think young man deserves his due."

"Are you for real?" Charlie figured if the guy was going to give him guff, he's better take it as well.

Carl touched his face, arm, and patted his abdomen. "Yup."

Bill came over to the table after waiting on a customer who continued to stand at the counter glaring directly at Charlie. Bill looked a little bewildered and shaken. Charlie knew the Evan's brothers from childhood. They were never really allowed to spend a lot of time with him, but his brothers were a different story. By that association, he knew them well enough to recognize the look. Bill was nervous and looked like he didn't know what to say.

"Hello sir," Bill held his hand out to Carl averting his eyes from Charlie. "May I help you with something?"

Bill's formality toward Carl and dismissal of himself seemed uncharacteristic to Charlie, so he looked over toward the counter where the man still stood tapping his foot, a scornful look toward their group and in particular toward Charlie.

If Carl noticed he didn't let on. "Hi, it's nice to meet you too sir. I'm actually looking for work and wondered if you had some customers looking for a good carpenter or would mind giving my name out. I can show you some of my work if you like." He reached around to his back pocket and pulled out some folded papers. "They're just drawings for now," his tone apologetic. "Maybe I can do some work for another carpenter until I prove myself. Do you know of anyone?"

"Yes certainly." Bill seemed relieved. "In fact, the man standing at the counter is looking for someone to redesign his private railcar. He's a little upscale if you don't mind working in those circumstances."

"I'll certainly give it a try. What gave me away as a carpenter?

"The hammer in your belt did."

"Oh, well why don't you introduce us?" He politely excused himself from Charlie and Jack, once again shaking hands with both. "Don't forget me on that cot there Jack."

Charlie would have loved to eaves drop on the conversation at the counter. He didn't dare, especially in front of Jack. Ma would be angry at him for a poor example. The man seemed to take forever, but finally left the store with his nose in the air like a dog sniffing the air for prey. In fact his face had a bulldog look about it. Bill returned with a message from Carl that he would be at the boarding house the next day to see about the loft. Bill had given him the address.

"So, have the two of you decided on your pattern."

"I have," Jack jumped in shoving the bed and cot instructions at Bill.

"Oh?"

"Yes, we want these for single beds or if we put the footboard on they can stack!" He pointed at the example on the front of the booklet. "We want this cot too for Carl. He likes barns. He actually asked if he could have the loft in our barn."

"He's a simple kind of guy isn't he?" Bill winked at Jack. "Okay well," he looked at Charlie who nodded. "Your brother seems to have a good mind for design."

"He sure does I'm proud to say. His choices look like winners. How much lumber do we need?"

Charlie and Bill figured out the amount of pine lumber, nails, pegs, and canvas for the mattresses. After tallying up the bill Charlie was left with a dollar and some change which he left on credit knowing they would need more materials.

"Who was the other gentleman?"

"He's the fella I told you about who might be interested in one of your open rooms."

"I didn't like the look of him. He seemed too self absorbed the way he glared at us and tapped his foot. Hum, well, we'd better get going, right Jack? We have a bunch of work to do."

"Yup!" Jack's shoulders went back and his chest out like a young soldier.

Charlie thought the boy acted a little young for his age, then he thought maybe he'd just been overshadowed by his older brothers too long." He smiled and looked at Bill. "I'll bring the buckboard back as soon as we unload it."

"Sounds like a good deal Charlie. Jack, do you want to take your wagon out to the yard with this ticket. Just give it to Jerry and he'll load you up." Bill shuffled his feet and looked around the store. He didn't look directly at Charlie.

"Jack, go ahead and get the order."

"I'll do a good job, Charlie." Jack took the order slip and left to get the lumber.

"Alright Bill, out with it, what did that guy say to you to upset you like this."

"Upset? I'm not upset; I'm just a little out of sorts today I guess."

"You didn't seem out of sorts when I got here."

"Dammit Charlie, this is my store and that's my business. Let it go. You have plenty to worry about in your own corner of town."

"I see." Charlie left the store feeling put in his place. He didn't usually get that feeling with the few people he did associate with. However, more and more since father's death he felt like his brown skin got darker. He could feel the prickle of hair rising on the back of his neck as if haunted by something that hadn't yet happened.

Chapter 5: Mr. Beal 1908

"Vernie, I don't want to do fours, and I don't want to do big words like softball. I want to play softball." Charlie heard Earl yelling at his sister. He started to get up from the desk.

Charlie sat in the den with his mother taking a well earned break when the noise started. He stood up ready to go remedy the problem for Vernie.

"Charlie, stay out of it or he'll never learn to respect her. If she chooses to ask for help, then it will be with her own authority and choice." She kept her voice low so the kids couldn't hear, but it didn't seem necessary with the noise Earl was making. It wasn't long before the whole makeshift classroom erupted. The 'classroom' was more often the family's living area where they could be away from all the responsibilities of the boarding house.

"Earl, be good. I have to do words and sums too! I like doing them." Pearl's six year old voice still held that sweet, little girl, sing song when she spoke.

"Shut up Pearl, all you do is cat, fat, hat. You have easy stuff. Vernie, I'm going to run out that door. I swear I will."

"Done," twelve year old Roy spoke up. "I finished the test. What was my time Vernie?"

Vernie's laugh filtered through the house. "How did you manage that with all Earl's hollering? You finished in twenty minutes. I was a minute test! Did you do a good job on it?"

"I think I did a good job. Earl didn't bother me because I put cotton in my ears. I could still hear him though so I guess I just turned him off."

"See there Earl. You want to holler, we can just turn you off until you decide to do your work and behave."

"I said I was going to walk out. You better be good to me Vernie."

"Earl sit down. You leave here without my dismissing you, and ma will whoop you. Now, finish that page of sums, and then we'll work on your compound words."

Lula started to snicker first, and then Charlie couldn't help but get caught up in the mirth. Vernie won the battle all on her own.

The day for changing rooms and setting up the new beds arrived. They placed Carl's cot in the barn loft the day after they met at the lumber yard. His cot was easy enough to build and he made good on his promise to clear the stall every day. He also helped build the bunks in his off time.

The two back rooms on the first floor became bedrooms for the family, making the entire second floor available for boarders.

The first, a widow and her daughter, moved into one of the doubles. The unfortunate woman had lost her husband to influenza and couldn't keep their farm. Her little girl looked about Earl's age.

A few days later another woman, new to the town, took up one half of a room with one of the current boarders. They seemed to have chosen each other, a great relief to Lula who enjoyed the banter of other women for a change. Charles would smile as he went by the parlor full of women tatting, knitting, and hand stitching and chatting as if they'd been great friends for years. It was a side of his mother he hadn't seen. He was glad to see her take some time out of her day.

She smiled much more around the house. One of the women, Mrs. Fry, considered herself somewhat of a gourmet cook and enjoyed tussling with Lula over who would cook the evening meal. Lula often let Mrs. Fry win.

Jack surprised them all with an interest in helping Mrs. Fry. He actually liked learning the tricks of her craft.

"Jackie the cook," they teased him, but only once in front of Lula.

They had one room left open, hoping to fill it with two more boarders. Charlie was taken back when he came home after an evening of gambling to find the room rented to Mr. Beal who insisted on the entire room to himself. Before he asked after the new arrival he went to the barn. "Carl, are you up there?"

"Yea, what's up?"

"Your boss is up at my house. He's already rented a room. Didn't he just have you rebuild his railcar?"

"Lordamercy, your ma is in for trouble, and so are you my friend."

Charlie had never seen his friend so agitated. "Oh lordamercy, I rebuilt a railcar alright. It wasn't anything fancy and it didn't even belong to the guy." Carl glared at the air as if Beal sat in front of him on a bale of hay that he kicked with a violence Charlie hadn't expected. "He bought an old broken down car from the railroad, set it in a field and wanted me to turn it into some kind of three story mansion for peanuts." Carl's anger at the man's 'con' as he called it seemed to seep green ooze through the walls of the barn. The horse Trotter even kicked at his stall.

"Whoa, better calm down man. He's really that bad?"

"Let me put it this way, you may have one of the devils minions renting a room."

Charles felt Carl may be going a bit far with his last remark. He snickered "Jeez, did you really just say he's a devil's minion."

Carl calmed. "Well, maybe that's a bit far, but not much. He seems all sweetness and gentleman like when it suits him, but the man is as cheap as they come. He didn't pay the lumber yard and he never paid me a dime for all the work I did. He said it wasn't what he wanted at all. He got drunk and burned it down one night. Then, to top it all off the owner of the field showed up madder than hell wondering how the thing got there in the first place."

"Man, why didn't you tell me this before? How did you hold it in so long? I would have been stomping around and yelling for days." He shook his head. "I'm going to have to talk with ma about this. She'll turn him out on his cheap ass real quick."

"Don't count on it."

"Why, ma listens to me."

"You'll see; that man has an effect on people."

He found his mother in the laundry room, washing linens the next morning. She had piles of clothing stacked around the floor awaiting her attention.

"Hi son, you're just in time. As soon as I finish rinsing and ringing these sheets, I'd like you to put them out on the line."

"Not a problem mother."

"Uh oh, you only call me mother when it's serious. What is it son?"

"Can you stop for a minute so we can really talk?"

She finished the last sheet. They went to the well worn kitchen table in the next room, while she dried her hands on that ever present, shoulder towel.

"Okay son, I'm listening."

He knew then he had her full attention. "Ma, it's this Mr. Beal. I don't trust him. Carl had some dealings with the man that turned out bad, not just for Carl but a few other people this guy shafted. I think he should go."

"Oh dear, Charlie I understand your misgivings. Mr. Beal told me about the problems he had with Carl and that farmer. It seems there was some misunderstanding and he's paying the farmer back for the damages. He said he's also making installments to the Evan's boys for any cost he has left. He's trying to do the right thing son."

"You really think that ma?"

"Why would he tell me so much if he was trying to hide it?"

"Well for one thing he wants to sell his story before you hear the truth from others, and he probably has something else up his sleeve. Carl thinks he's very devious."

"Oh that's silly. Carl thinks he has reason to be angry I'm sure. He just didn't do the work as he was asked is all. Mr. Beal said he paid him for half of his time."

"And you believe that."

"Of course, he seems like a perfectly charming gentleman. Earl and Pearl have certainly taken to him."

Charles dropped the subject for fear of pushing his mother more to Beal's side, but he intended to find out more. He walked to the lumber yard. Bill Evans may feel more like explaining his reaction to the man that had cheated him out of money. Besides, Bill probably knew the town as good as anyone and whoever else Beal may have cheated.

Bill was stacking some lumber he'd just brought in from the mill. Charlie saw him as he walked by the fenced yard. "Hey Bill, who's watching the store?"

"Ah, hey Charlie, look here how much help this buckboard is already. I rigged up a hitch for the back of the truck and she's followin' along behind like a dream. Sure glad you stopped in that day."

"I'm glad the buckboard worked for you. It makes me feel good that we didn't just waste it." Charlie found the open gate and helped Bill unload what was left.

"Thanks Charlie, the piles are looking good ain't they?"

"They're well stacked. Ma would have you organize her kitchen if she saw. I would never have thought to fix a truck hitch to that buckboard. You're turning out to be some kind of genius." Charlie snickered. "I may just have to get me one of them vehicles. That way I could take mom and the kids out for some nice drives around the countryside."

"Wow that sounds nice. Sure beats hooking up the horse and that boxy little wagon you left yourself with."

"Well, that's true for fun rides, not so much for hauling though."

"Hey, Bill what's taking you so long out there? I'd kind of like to go to Bueller's for a nice hot lunch."

"Only if you bring me back somethin'."

"Hey Charlie, how ya doin" They were in the store by then. There were no customers around so they could talk without any fear of being overheard.

"I'm doing fine Jerry, but I kind of wanted to ask you two about Mr. Beal. I've always known since that first day something was off with him. Now he's moved into the boarding house and has all the women and little kids eating out of his hand. Ma won't listen. She says he's a fine, charming gentleman and I need to quit worrying. Carl paints a whole different picture."

"That scoundrel shouldn't ever show his face in here again! I owe you an apology for the way I acted that day. You traded me that buckboard in good faith. He had me convinced he was some high society gent. He didn't much like being in the store with a black man." Bill took a breath. "Charlie, I refused to ask you to leave, but he convinced me he was going to bring in a lot of repeat business, so I got all nose in the air to ya. Then I heard all that stuff he did. What an idiot. I don't know who the worst idiot is; me for believing him or him for thinking he'd pull it off."

Charlie had wanted to stop Bill's apologies, but he needed to know about Beal.

"Well he's still trying to pull something off. I don't like the way he flirts with ma. What's worse is she seems to like it."

"I hope she comes to her senses. Jerry won't like it much when he sees the guy over there. Maybe he'll tell your ma about the guy and she'll kick Beal out."

"Well, who knows, I don't see Jerry making a fuss at the table, but I don't know how he will react when he sees Beal either."

"Yup, it's kinda sticky isn't it? Hey, how about games while the store's empty, not a game of chance mind you, but maybe a good game of gin rummy for the fun of it." Bill cajoled.

They cleared the table and Bill dealt. Nobody came in the store until after one o'clock. "We should just close from noon to one. Your ma's cooking draws a great deal of the customers."

"Well, I'll have to get onto her about that." Charlie smiled as a look of horror crossed Bill's face.

"Oh, don't you dare. I love your ma's cookin' and if she closes those noon meals..," He stopped when he heard Charlie laughing. "Okay, just for that my friend, Gin." He lay the cards out in a flourish placing them on the table like a fan.

Jerry came back with a basket of chicken, corn on the cob, and cherry pie.

"Charlie, you tell your ma thank you for this. Now you see why I don't want her shutting down her lunches."

"As if she would,"

"No, but she should be more concerned with who sits at her table. Mr. Beal was there acting all full of himself and flirting with all the ladies. He seemed most interested in your mother Charlie." Jerry added.

"Yes, I know he's taken a room. He's a steam engine going full speed toward ma, and I can't seem to get him stopped. At least now I can tell my mother about him swindling so many people. How did he stay out of jail anyway?"

"The sheriff warned him if he caused any more trouble, Beal would be arrested. He's also supposed to pay everyone back. "

"So has he?"

"Just about a nickel so far, but the sheriff says it shows good faith." Jerry injected

"Ha, that's a laugh." Bill spat into a spittoon at the end of counter though he didn't chew tobacco. "We just have a lazy sheriff."

Chapter 6: Pearl

Charlie waited for a chance to tell his mother about Beal's misdeeds. It wasn't until several days later that he found her alone doing laundry.

"Hi son, would you hand me that pile of dungarees, and then get the shirts off the line? They should be dry by now." She took a deep breath and smiled. "I love the smell of fall. The squash are ripe for canning and the harvest is coming in."

"It does smell delicious ma." Charles handed her the dungarees one pair at a time. "Ma, I need to talk to you about Mr. Beal. I don't think you should trust the guy."

"Charlie, what is your problem. He's been perfectly sweet and proper."

"He's nice enough when you're around. He's cheated just about everyone in town. Just ask Carl or the Evan's boys."

She seemed to think for a minute. "He told me he'd made a mess of his start here in Wyman. Poor dear, he wanted to sound better than he was. The sheriff thinks he deserves a second chance. He told me he made a payment to the lumber yard already."

There was nothing more Charlie could have said then. He had to wait and hope Beal showed his own hand. "Okay ma, I'll get those shirts."

"What am I supposed to do Carl? Beal heads me off at every turn. He's all nice when ma's around, but when she's out of sight he brags that he's going to get ma to marry him and then get rid of me."

"I don't know friend. I don't think your ma will be as easy as Beal thinks. I don't think she's thinking about marriage to anyone."

"And you would know that how?"

Carl chuckled. "I heard her say so to Vernie the other day. Vernie asked her if she was going marry Mr. Beal. Your ma said she wasn't thinking about marrying anybody."

Two days later a high pitched scream rang through the house. "Pearl! Somebody get me some ice, this baby is burning up." They could hear the harsh, croupy cough throughout the house.

By the time Charlie dressed and got out of his bedroom, Vernie rushed by him with a pan of ice chunks. Tears ran down her face. Without a word he ran to Dr. Wilson's house.

Mrs. Wilson opened the door wrapped in a flannel robe, auburn hair in curlers. "Charlie, what's wrong?"

"Pearl, I think its croup."

"Doc!" she yelled and he appeared dressed, bag in hand within seconds.

"Don't look so shocked Charlie; I've always got some clothes at the end of the bed and my doctor bag right beside them. I also know Mrs. Wilsons call. Let's go."

Nobody could go into or near the sick room. Earl banged on the door. "I want Pearl!" The two children were companions who fought, played and banded together to torment their older siblings. "Don't let her die like Daddy Charlie." Tears choked the child, and Charlie felt his own throat tighten. What can I say Early B.? I want' to tell you it's okay. Dear God, why are you taking my family?"

"Come one Early B. why don't we go for a ride on trotter? Any small way Charlie could distract him the better. As head of the family, he did everything in his power to stay calm for the, but he was jelly inside.

Exhausted, he found Carl in the barn cleaning Trotter's stall.

"Hey Charlie, I'm sure sorry to hear Pearl's sick. She's such a sweet thing." He propped the pitchfork against the wall and took Trotter's reins from Charlie."

Charlie watched in silence while Carl unsaddled the horse, removed his bridle and brushed him down. Tough and ever sensitive Carl could have been a preacher, helping his congregation if he wasn't given to liquor and poker.

"Let it go friend. You're a man not a piece of iron."

Charlie looked up at Carl shocked. "What?"

"I watch you dear friend. I see you taking care of Earl, fixing it for everyone but yourself. Take a breath!"

A deep moan escaped Charlie as he bent over double. His gut felt on fire and his head pounded. "Damn you Carl! Why couldn't you just let me be strong? I have to hold together you idiot." He retched until what little his body could squeeze from his stomach foamed on the dirt floor, leaving at wet patch of mud. Tears ran down his cheeks from the effort, and from fatigue. "Why can't I protect them? It's my job to see that everything is safe, but this croup, I can't fight that away." Charlie laid his face in his hands, shoulders jerking with his sobs. It was only then he could find relief even for a few moments.

Then the tearing sound of a mother's scream ripped the air. Not Pearl, my Pearl!"

"Let me come with you. Don't try to handle this by yourself."

Charlie nodded mechanically.

"I don't know Carl. It's all gone. I have nothing left and I know ma is just as exhausted."

"That's why you are going to let me take a part in this Charlie. I love your family and I think they kind of like me. I can help."

Mrs. Wilson came out of the kitchen with a basin full of damp rags, and Pearl's little white christening dress. "Charlie, I'm sorry we lost Pearl."

"I know, Mrs. Wilson, we heard the scream from the barn." Carl spoke for his friend.

"Carl," She sobbed. "Charlie has a great friend in you."

"Yes I do." Charlie responded. His head didn't seem to want to come up, but he knew they were there.

"I have a great friend in Charlie, and his family."

She smiled, "Take your friend in the kitchen and make him drink some coffee. Perk him up. We've got this all under control for now."

The house itself seemed to weep. Earl was inconsolable and though Lula tried, she couldn't seem to fulfill his need for comfort. Charlie took him for buggy rides and walks in the park. Earl almost nine now was old enough to understand death's permanent nature. He also feared for his own survival.

"Charlie," Lula called from the den piling three satchels on a table against the wall. "I need to have you stay here and take care of the boarding house while I take Pearl to be buried with her father and grandparents. I know it must be hard for you son, but I can't think about this place until my baby is taken care of. I I I'm sorry." She broke down in tears and Charles couldn't help shedding some himself as he held her to his chest. Seeing his mother distraught made him feel useless. All he could do was hold her until she decided enough was enough.

"I'm okay now son." She pressed her dress with her hands and went to the kitchen to start some kind of meal, but Mrs. Fry stopped her by carrying a huge tureen of soup from the kitchen just before Lula got to the door.

"Oh my," Mrs. Fry exclaimed. "I almost ran right into you Lula. Why don't you get your family to the table? I already have a basket of fresh warm bread and some crackers in there.

There had been no open lunch for the public since Pearl took ill, yet friends continued to bring food, prepared dishes ready for a hand to simply warm them up. Such was what Mrs. Fry had done.

Charlie ate in silence, thinking of Pearl. He was much older, but he'd always remember that sweet little girl's smile, her teasing when she wanted him to give her a piggy back ride, or her singing and dancing circles around the living room floor. The floors always had a high polish that allowed a little girl in stocking feet to twirl and slide.

"Charlie, do you mind staying while we take Pearl back to Blue Rivers?"

'No, mother I'll say my goodbyes before you leave. I don't want anyone bothered because of that ridiculous funeral director. He didn't seem to learn the first time and after the Grandparent's funerals, I don't feel like stepping foot in that town again."

"I'm sorry son. I know how badly that hurts you."

"I could tend to the boarding house for you if Charlie here would like to go. A big brother should be at his baby sister's funeral."

Mr. Beal's offer almost made Charles sick. "No thank you Mr. Beal. I will stay and take care of everything here." The man's gall and false sincerity made Charlie want to punch him then and there, but he couldn't. Beal managed to twist his way into the good graces of Charlie's mother any way he could.

"Excuse me ma, I don't feel hungry. I'll talk to you later about the arrangements."

"That sounds fine son." Her voice sounded lifeless.

Charles knew she didn't really hear what he said. She was despondent and there was nothing he could do for her. Vernie cried endlessly. Jack and Roy spent as much time outside as they could. They would swing on the old wooden swing under the walnut tree, but their heads were low. Occasionally someone might laugh for just a moment. Charles focused his attention on Earl, putting him to bed at night, making sure he dressed and washed up every day. On the evening before the family would leave for Blue Rivers, Charles learned Beal intended to accompany the family in his place. There was nothing he could do, but make his own position as head of the Bueller clan plain.

"Ma, I would like to oversee the loading of the casket onto the train. It's the least I can do for my baby sister." He'd emphasized the word 'my' for Beal's sake, but the man seemed unaffected.

"Son, you are the only one I would trust that to." Charlie and his mother looked into each other's eyes and a message of shared sorrow passed between them. He could see Beal cringe out of the corner of his eye as he turned to attend to the casket. Beal better not mess with me today. I don't have the time or care to deal with that SOB.

Just as the small casket slid safely into the railcar, Charlie heard Beal's voice behind him.

"Well now, you are her favorite son aren't you?"

"Stay away from me, and get the hell away from my mother."

"What are you going to do about it boy? Favorite son or not, I have you out maneuvered. I can't see why she'd keep a black whelp in the first place, or why she's so taken to you. I'll have you out of that house and your ma in my bed before you know it."

Charlie drew back his arm ready to swing when Carl caught it from behind. "Mr. Beal you cheated me and about everybody else around here. Mrs. Bueller is a good woman and you are a scoundrel. Next time I won't stop Charlie."

Somehow, Charlie felt Carl made the biggest impact on Beal. Not because of color, but Carl's ability to sound composed, and quietly sinister.

Beal stomped off in a temper, but he stopped short of sight of the passenger car with the family. He took a deep breath, smoothed his suit jacket, straightened his tie and looked back at Charlie and Carl as he turned on a smile like a lighting a candle.

"Did you see that? How do I fight that?"

"Charlie, I wish I knew. I've never come across anyone so devious before."

Chapter 7: A New Year

As 1909 dawned, it became apparent that Lula looked at Mr. Beal as more than a boarder.

Throughout the previous year Charles had watched the relationship grow. It started with Beal being attentive after Pearl's death. Charles saw the man hang by Lula's side and pull her head to his shoulder whenever she got sad. When Charles tried to speak alone with his mother about the boarding house, Beal made himself available to give 'sage' advice.

Since Pearl's death Charlie's relationship with Earl seemed to wane and Beal slipped smoothly into the void. Earl seemed to gravitate toward his need for a father. Charlie knew he was losing the battle for his family to Beal.

The fact that they lived under the same roof made the situation more impossible. By the end of January, he'd built a cot and moved into the other half of the barn loft.

"Get all settled?" Carl called from across a stack of hay bales between them.

"Yea, this is a lot warmer and comfortable up here than I expected." His cot fit like a sling hugging his six foot, two hundred ten pound frame. He pulled two hefty quilts over him.

"Did you know you snore?" Charlie startled when Carl shook him.

"What do you want?" It took time to clear his head enough to remember he was in the loft. "Damn Carl, I was sleeping like a baby, for once."

"I noticed, I haven't had a wink of sleep yet. You snore my friend. Try turning on your side or something."

Charlie scooted and twisted until he was on his side. It took a minute for his body to feel accustomed to the feel of the canvas. Thankfully, he'd made it almost twice as wide as the pattern called for, just as he had Carl's. He finally slipped back into a comfortable sleep.

***

"You can't let her marry him son." Henry's torn body appeared as it was the day of his fall from the platform. *"He'll kill me again."*

"What can I do pa. Look at you. You're all torn and dead. I miss you so much. It's been really hard since you left."

"I see you my Charlie. I can't come back to help you, but please don't let that man take over what your ma and I built."

"I'll try pa." Charles saw his father's body heal in front of his eyes. *The rending of his side reversed as bones mended, muscles knitted back to their normal form, and the skin covered it all perfectly without a single scar.*

"I trust you son. Who be Charlie B?"

"I be Charlie B. pa."

***

Charles woke with a start. "Pa!"

"Slow down there buddy. You had a kind of rough time waking up." Carl laced up his boots as he sat on a bale between their divided lofts. "Bad dream?"

"Odd more than anything, I saw pa and he wants me to keep Beal away from ma. How do I do that with the way Beal is always ahead of me."

"For one thing, it was a dream. You don't have the ability to control your mother, so unless you can get him to show his real self in her presence, I don't think you can do much." Carl sat looking at his friend pull on his pants over his long johns. "Can I ask you something personal without making you angry?"

"You're always in my personal stuff Carl, mostly by my own invitation."

"How much experience have you had with women?"

A dark head snapped up, but with a puzzled rather than angry look. "Well, only with the girls down at the saloon. They like to flirt with everyone."

"So between the two of us, we have almost no experience with women at all. I mean I had a gal I thought was kind of special back in

Missouri, but nothing more 'n that."

"Missouri?"

"I grew up in the Dakota's for a while, and then I moved south and landed in Missouri, but we're not getting into that now."

"What are you saying?"

"Beal has an advantage of knowing how to court a woman, and especially how to sweet talk lonely women like your momma. That's shoes you can't fill. I think maybe you should stop trying before you make trouble between you and your ma."

Charlie didn't want to talk about it anymore. He wanted to be anywhere but Wyman at that moment. Too much had happened and too few opportunities for a man like him. Whenever he thought about the past few years he felt like jumping on a train track in front of a fast train.

Breakfast didn't go much better.

"Lula, let me clear that away for you. You've been through enough my dear." Beal made a flourish of his chivalry.

"Uh hum, Ma where is Vernie? I've kind of been missing her around here."

"Oh Charlie, I'm sorry I forgot to tell you. She went back to Blue Rivers to stay with my cousin. I'm not sure she's coming back son. She's not sure what to do right now."

"I know how she feels."

It was about then Roy and Earl showed up in the kitchen. "Who is going to do our lessons?" Roy asked.

"There is that school up the road a bit. I think you could both do well there. You'll like the teacher."

"Who is the teacher?" Earl jumped in.

"I am." The widow lady spoke up, Charles felt bad he didn't know all their names. "With the two of you and my daughter Isabella, we will finally have twelve students."

"Early B., I think that sounds like a good idea."

"Charlie, you don't have to call me Early B. anymore. I'm nine years old."

"Nine! Wow you grew all the way up to almost a man." Charlie tried to tease, but the scornful look on his brother's face made him think twice. "Okay Earl, you are right. It's time I started treating all of you boys like young men. After school you, Jack and Roy can help me pick out some good patching shingles for the barn roof. I noticed we have some light coming through and some snow falling into the loft."

"It's too cold Charlie." Earl whined and Roy nodded.

"Hmm, I thought you were growing up?"

"Charlie!"

"Okay ma, but if they put on their coats, galoshes and gloves, they can help for a while. It won't take that long." It wasn't so much a matter of what needed to be done as the training of young boys to start being young men, something Charlie felt he'd been neglecting.

"Okay, I agree with your brother. Roy and Earl, the two of you can bundle up and help for a while."

"What does Jack do?"

"I got a job down and the rail yard. They need a switchman and it pays good."

"Thank goodness somebody is getting a job around here." Beal jumped in.

Lula glared at him. "Mr. Beal you are still a boarder here and I'll thank you not to interfere with my family."

Charlie couldn't hide a smile. Ma still saw fit to put the man in his place.

"I have to take off for my own job. I'm helping a new family estimate the cost of building a new house. I'm just glad to get some work out of season." Carl nodded to the ladies and left for the day.

The younger boys went back inside after about an hour. Beal caught Charlie outside on a ladder pulling snow off the barn roof, and shook the ladder threatening to make the young man fall.

"Hey you idiot, that's not funny at all. Are you trying to kill me or something?"

"Let's just say it's something, Bueller. Don't ever try to come between me and your ma."

Charlie jumped from the fifth rung of the ladder to face Bueller. "I just want you to remember one thing Beal."

"What's that?"

"Remember this next time you make moves on my family." Charlie didn't have Carl to catch his arm this time, but he did have the calm to be careful where he placed the blow. He thrust his fist up into Beal's stomach causing the old man to bend forward over the offending arm gagging. "That was a warning." To punctuate his meaning, he stepped behind Beal and placed a foot on his backside sending the older man face first into the snow.

Chapter 8: Meeting with George

Beal managed to beat Charlie in the next set up. He'd confessed to goading Charlie 'a bit' to which the younger punched him and summarily dropped him in the snow. Lula was livid when she saw her eldest son. He'd crossed a line in her eyes, and since he seemed to play into Beal's hand at every turn, Charlie decided temporary retreat his best course.

Fred returned for a couple of months over the holidays that year. "Oh brother, am I glad to see you! We've made a lot of changes since you left."

"Charlie, I can't tell you how hard it was for me when I heard the news about little Pearl. I didn't get the telegram for a full week after the funeral. I'll bet ma was really mad at me."

"I think she was so full of grief, holding herself together to make plans and make the trip was all she could handle. I'm sure she'd like to hear from you now though."

"I sent her a letter about the whole thing. Pearl was so sweet and young. I heard Vernie went to Kansas."

"Yes, she couldn't seem to bring herself to come back here. She'd been teaching the children their lessons. I don't think she could face that little class. Earl and Roy are finishing at a new school up the road. One of our boarders is teaching there.

Fred's long gait was difficult to keep up with as they walked from the railroad station. His arms hung to about four inches above his knees and that gave him an advantage during fights. If anyone bore the Greek physique in the Bueller family, Fred's profile made the best example.

"Who's this Mr. Beal I keep hearing about?"

"You'll meet him soon enough."

"Hey, did that sign say what I thought. Is that the Evan's boys we grew up with?"

"It sure is. Their pa still has the saw mill so the brothers keep well stocked on lumber and hardware. We built a bunch of new bunks and two cots for the loft."

The two visited the Evan's Lumber and most of the other stores on their way home. Fred picked their mother a silk scarf at the mercantile. "You're making it big in the fighting game I hear." The shop owner remarked. "Who would have thought one of our own boys would grow up to be a prize fighter."

"Well, I'm not quite there yet, but I'm getting closer."

"Those long arms of yours will send you straight to the top. I saw a guerrilla with arms like that once." The three laughed and Jack slouched, hanging his arms low acting like a monkey from the circus.

"I saw a circus years back in Beatrice. I think they'll be back this way in a year or two. Have you ever been to a circus Charlie?"

"Nope, but we did go see the parade once. They had what they called a chimpanzee there. Fred looks a lot like it." Laughter rang through the store.

"The great white chimp, I guess it's better than chump." Fred imitated the animal. "Maybe you should take the part Charlie."

"Oh, yeah?" They stood close enough to compare arm length. "Seems I come up a bit shorter brother, take that." Charlie punched Fred in the arm.

The shop owner stepped up and grabbed their shoulders. "Okay boys, there's too much merchandise for you to be breaking up my store." He laughed.

"Yeah, I'll take him down a peg or so in the barn at home." Fred smirked.

"I'd rather arm wrestle you Fred. I'm not that dumb to try to get inside those noodle arms of yours."

"I do have a smart brother."

"Okay you two; that sounds just fine to me." The owner sighed. "Now will you please tell your ma we're getting a library committee together. We're going to have our own honest to goodness public library before long."

"That sounds wonderful. Ma loves to read and to tell you the truth, I kind of like reading those Mark Twain books and Edgar Allan Poe. I think we even have some books we could help get it started with.

"Well, if I come across any in Omaha who want to donate a few books, I'll bring some next time I'm back." Fred announced.

"This town doesn't appreciate the Bueller's enough family has given a lot for this town."

The brothers left the store with Fred's package wrapped in pretty paper with a nice pink ribbon.

Supper was a grand time that evening. Mrs. Fry and Lula put on a holiday spread even though they were in between Thanksgiving and Christmas. Fred handed Lula his gift and protested that she open it right away and not wait for Christmas day. Her eyes gleamed as she carefully unfolded the silk scarf with delicate pink roses surrounded by green. It was a long time since she'd looked so happy. In fact, since Pearls death not even Mr. Beal had been able to make her smile like that.

She kissed Fred on the cheek. "Son, I will always treasure this."

Beal, not to be outdone scooted his chair back, got onto one knee and declared his undying love in front of the entire room and asked Lula to marry him. Not many in the room seemed as shocked as the three men setting grouped around the opposite end of the table. Carl, Fred, and Charlie all looked at each other in disbelief, but even that couldn't match the looks on their faces when she accepted.

Fred recovered first, not knowing the man as Carl and Charlie did. "Well, I guess congratulations are in order. Mr. Beal I don't believe I've heard your first name."

"Oh, thank you Fred. It's Oliver. My mother loved to read Oliver Twist by that Dickens fellow and named me for that little scamp in the book, if I remember he gave the head of the orphanage a bit of trouble."

"Only by some Mr. Beal, Lula corrected. Oliver was quite a nice child and grew up to be a kind young man."

"Hmm, I kind of like that, thanks my dear."

Charlie and Carl made their way out the door and to the barn. It wasn't long until Fred joined them.

"Fred, we have got to talk to George. At least we need to know what this man might be able to take once they're married."

"I agree Charlie. I didn't much like the way he horned in. He's a little too pushy for my taste. I'll ride Trotter to Beatrice and call on George and his new bride tomorrow."

"New bride, I thought they'd been married a while. Didn't I see the announcement in the paper a year ago?"

"Yeah, I guess I still consider that new. Nevertheless, whatever George's problem is with our family, he can at least give a little free legal advice for Ma's sake."

Fred left the next morning. Charlie's insides were wiggling like he was full of worms waiting for him to get back. He decided to build a small wagon for Earl. The kid needed something to occupy him and he could help by hauling small loads for the others.

89

Evan's lumber was open. "Hey Bill, I'm making a pull wagon for Earl. I need four tires, something for axles and a wagon pull." He'd walked in looking for a hammer for Jack. He didn't bother to look to the back of the store where the checkout counter stood.

"Well, Charlie I guess you'll have to wait your turn here." Bill's tone was impatient.

Charlie noticed one of the town's elders at the counter.

"Sorry, I meant no disrespect. I'm a little wound up and didn't see you there Mr., um, I'm sorry I can't remember your name at the moment. I'll just take a look around." He couldn't remember the man's name, so Mr. would have to do.

"My name is Sir to you, boy."

Charlie controlled his anger. More and more he felt unwelcome even in Wyman.

Bill finished his transaction with 'Sir' and the man left with his purchase.

"Okay Charlie. Sorry the he said what he did, but you do need to expect other customers."

"I know, I know. I'm just tired of the way everyone's been treating me since pa's not around anymore."

"Not everyone Charlie. I think of myself as a friend and I know Jerry does too. A few good friends is better than a bunch of back stabbing types."

"You mean like Beal."

"You said it not me." Bill pulled out a notepad and pencil. "Let's figure out what you need. I do have small wooden wagons for kids."

"How much are those?"

"Well, take a look. I have this red one for a dollar. If you want the high sides for it, that's quite a bit extra. That's where they get you is on the accessories."

"I think I'll just take the red wagon. Do you suppose I should get something for the others?"

"I think you need to answer that for yourself. It's not Christmas. Here, I've got some licorice I could throw in, or some peppermint sticks."

"Give me about ten of those peppermint sticks. Do I still have enough on credit to get jack a hammer? I'll just get the wagon for both Earl and Roy. But I will take the peppermint sticks."

"This is really hard on you isn't it. I can't imagine having to suddenly look after so many people."

"I can handle the kids, it's Beal that's going after ma, and I don't think he is doing it for love. I think he wants to get his hands on the boarding house."

"Can he do that?"

"Fred went to Beatrice to ask George. I hope we can call Beal out on it. I hope ma will see him for who he is. Well, I need to get home and hide this in the barn. Thanks, I think the kids all deserve something for all they've been through."

Charles managed to get the wagon into the barn and covered with a horse blanket and straw before the boys got home from school. He would give it to them later. Roy could still appreciate a red wagon. There was a noise of hoorahs from the house. It seemed someone started a party without him. The moment he stepped in the front door his mother grabbed him by the arm.

"Oh Charlie, please be happy for me. Oliver thought it would be best if we got married right away. It makes sense Charlie. We're going to get married anyway, so why not now."

"What?" Charlie choked out in a whisper and fell into a chair.

"Son?"

"Mother, I really don't want you to marry Beal. At least not until Fred gets back from Beatrice."

"What does that have to do with it?"

"He went to see George to find out what Beal might be able to take from you and the family once you're married."

"So you don't think he loves me. Charlie that is insulting. I'm not young anymore, but a man can still find me attractive." She paced back and forth wringing her hands. "Is this about your father? I know you miss him honey, and Oliver will never replace him in my heart."

"No, mother you're young enough I kind of expected you might get married again. I just don't trust Beal."

Tears filled Lula's eyes before she could turn away. His heart dropped, throat felt like a noose about to hang him for his crime of disapproving his mother's choice. "Mother, anyone can be taken in. This guy probably cons people for a living."

She stomped her foot hard on the wooden floor of the kitchen. "Well, I guess you'd better just go stay in the barn with Carl. You don't need to come to my wedding if that's the way you think about the man I love. I'm lonely Charlie and you need to understand that."

"Ma... I."

"Git." She pointed to the back door. Now there was nothing he could do even if Fred found out Beal could take it all. He'd shown his hand too soon and lost.

Fred returned within an hour. Charlie dreaded the answer and unfortunately he'd been right. Once his mother married Oliver Beal, he owned everything. She lost all rights of property to her husband.

"Damn Fred, it's too late. I tried to stop it, but they were getting ready for the wedding when I got back from Evan's Lumber. I went down to get Earl and Roy a small wagon. I figure they should have something since Pearl is gone, something that could draw them boys closer to each other."

"Charlie, you always think about the rest of us and how you can do everything to make our lives better. But today you are over thinking. Get your good clothes on and get to the house. I'm going to do the same. Unless we want to alienate ma completely, we need to show her we trust her judgment."

"Even if we don't?"

"Especially if we don't."

Chapter 9: What's Next?

Mrs. Fry outdid herself with the wedding reception. She decorated the dining table all in white with rose petal shaped confetti cut out of thin red and pink tissue paper. Charlie imagined all the women in the house finding some private spot and cutting dozens of the little decorations. Someone found a box of Christmas garland and pulled out the white and red to decorate the staircase.

Charlie counted five tiers on the cake, which Mrs. Fry and Jack decorated with white icing and some more of the confetti hearts and a big flower on top.

The ceremony was over. Charlie tried to be on his best manners and even congratulated both his mother and Beal. He felt so deflated he wanted to find a corner and cry like a small child. He didn't know how many more people he could stand to lose. His family was all he had. Except for Carl, he didn't know anyone who would see past his brown skin. He knew there would be a day of reckoning between him and Oliver Beal. However; at that moment he saw his mother as a vision of womanhood that was marrying a man she loved, not a mother. A small hat sat on the crown of her head with a little piece of netting at the front. Her ivory dress could have been sewn from one of her usual patterns, but it didn't look like anything he'd seen her wear before. "Mother, you look beautiful," he whispered.

Beal stood next to his five foot ten inch bride and looked dwarfed.

Not a tall man, the groom stood at her ear. Somehow that comforted Charlie. He shook Beal's hand, but there was no warmth from either of them. Beal's hand felt like one of his mother's noodles before it dried, cold and limp. Suddenly, Charlie knew it was the end of another relationship. He would no longer be the head of the family; the spot was taken by a scoundrel. He knew soon he would leave, but not until Jack and Roy were old enough and knew how to watch for any unscrupulous tells their new step father would show.

He would teach them poker the way his father taught him. They would learn to watch Beal for his a face or move he may make when he's cheating or lyingm what pa called a 'tell.'

"Hey brother, I see those gears going."

"Oh, I'm sorry I need to get my head out of the way for tonight don't I?"

"It might help you feel better. Hey, go get that wagon for the boys."

"Not exactly a wedding gift."

"Can you think of anything ma would like better?"

Charlie's smile seemed so white with his darker skin. Curling his long arm around Fred's shoulder he shook him lightly as he pulled him close. "You know what? You're pretty okay."

"Jeez, I'd hate to see what you do to me if I wasn't pretty okay."

They forgot the company and started laughing loud enough to be heard through the house. "Woops!" Charlie looked at his mother. "I'll be right back."

Five minutes later he pulled the wagon into the party room. "Roy, Early B. come here I have something for you, if that's okay with the wedding party."

"That's great with the wedding party son." Lula let the tears at the corners of her eyes show. Beal even smiled at him and nodded.

"Oh wow, lookit what we got Earl."

"Give me a ride first." The younger brother squealed.

"Outside with it boys," Lula held up her hand "after you go change into play clothes."

"Ah ma!."

The room erupted with laughter.

As night approached and the party broke up, Charlie couldn't think about his mother sharing her room with a scoundrel. He was glad to get back to his room in the loft.

"Hey Charlie, did you bring me anything from the wedding?"

Charlie started almost falling over the edge. "Carl, I forgot all about you. Jeez, you scared the crap out of me."

His friend clutched his chest, rolled his eyes into his head and flopped back on some hay bales, "Oh the betrayal!"

"If you're trying out for a part at the theater, I have news. I'm not the guy to audition to."

"Oh what tangled webs they weave. Ah, canst I persuade young squire for a scrap?"

"I think you can go in the door and find plenty to eat. You know ma looks at you like one of her own. Go wish her a happy wedding day." He flashed an insincere smile at his friend. "Oh, for the acting," He clapped his hands to reward his friend.

Carl bowed "I must take what tiny bits of favor you fain throw my way." Then he flitted off like a crippled ballet dancer. The sound of the ladder breaking, and then Carl's muscular frame cracking the floorboards below, made Charlie jump. He scrambled to the edge and hung over to see that his friend lay flat and unconscious on the floor. "Carl!"

He hung over the edge of the loft and dropped down beside Carl's still form checking the young   man for signs of life, he was glad to see his friend breathing. He could only see traces of blood in the straw. The jagged slivers of broken floor boards worried him most.

He ran to the house, "Ma, help!"

"Charlie?"

"It's Carl, he's in the barn. Is Dr. Wilson still here?"

"They went home a while ago." Mrs. Fry replied.

The wedding forgotten, Lula ran in her wedding clothes to the barn and Charlie ran across the street to Dr. Wilson.

Dr., Mrs. Wilson, and Charlie hustled into the barn.

"Lula, you haven't moved him at all have you?"

"No, I was waiting for some help to get him in the house."

"Whew!" Dr. Wilson s relief was telling. "I just need to check him and make sure his neck and back aren't broken."

"Oh dear God," Charles looked at his friend still unconscious, laid out like a ragdoll on the floorboards. "I can't handle this. I'm sorry." He ran around the side of the barn and vomited. *Man, why I do lose my guts every time things get stressful? Me and my damn stomach; grow the hell up Charlie and get back to your friend.*

"Oh good Charlie your back, I think Carl might need to lean on you to walk to the house. I'm going to observe from behind."

Carl sat up against a post with a couple of feed sacks behind for some degree of comfort.

"So his neck and back bone are okay?"

"I'm okay Charlie. No broken bones but I hurt like holy h."

"Now wait a minute, you do have a small fracture of your skull. You need to be watched and stay awake. I'll be checking your eyes every so often too."

"Golly doc. I guess I'm worse off than I thought."

"We just don't know yet."

"Shouldn't I just pick him up and carry him in?" Charlie asked.

"Actually Charlie, I want to watch his gait, so just support him don't bear his weight for him, okay? Make sure he doesn't get dizzy or faint and fall again."

"Okay Carl here we go." They hobbled into the kitchen to the table. Carl didn't' faint or complain about being dizzy.

"Well that's good. Lula, you go on to bed. This is your wedding night. Charlie and I will take care of this young man."

"Okay, if you want anything to eat, we have a lot left over."

"Carl was on his way in to get something when he fell. Can he have something to eat?"

"Do you think you want to try it?" Dr. Wilson asked his patient.

"Just a little something please, I think I smell some turkey if I could have a bit of that."

"Coming up," Charlie made him a plate with some turkey, and bread with butter.

Carl picked at it, but didn't seem interested in eating a lot. "I feel so tired."

"Nothing doing, I need you to stay awake. You probably have a concussion and if you start to have more problems I need to see those eyes."

"Fine, so what do I do?"

"Focus on your cards." Dr. Wilson ordered. Then nodded to Charlie; "Don't you have any cards?" .

"Well of course I do." Charlie reached in his back pocket and threw a deck on the table.

Chapter 10: Beal's Boarding House

"What's going on here? Damn, you have blood all over the kitchen floor." Beal grouched as he entered, obviously unaware of anything that transpired the night before. "What's wrong with Carl?"

"He fell from the loft in the barn. The ladder broke. Don't worry, I'll clean up the blood and check the damage to the barn in the morning."

"I'd prefer you clean it up now." Beal reached into the top cupboard, his short nightshirt rising up over his buttocks.

"I'll do it, don't worry. Right now Carl is all I care about."

"Well, Charlie it seems you have your priorities mixed up. You are living on my property, you do as I request."

"Get the hell out of here. This is my home, long before you hauled that saggy butt into it." Charlie had cleaned the small drops of blood off the floor by that time, but only so they wouldn't stain. He took a single aggressive step toward Beal landing his foot hard on the floor.

"That you will regret," Beal shuffled out of the kitchen with his coffee. Charlie couldn't help but laugh at the little man. "Did you see him? I think maybe I should check to see if he left a trail of piss."

Doc's voice was soft and firm. "Charlie, I'd tread carefully for now. That man has some kind of weird friendship with the sheriff."

They were so preoccupied they hadn't noticed Carl slump over the table and pass out. Charlie reached to grab his friends shoulder but Doc stopped him.

"Let's not rattle him anymore than he already is. From now on, I check his eyes, breathing and pulse. You push that bench out from the table and find something soft to put on them."

Charlie ran from the kitchen and came back with several pillows.

"He's still responding, but his eyes are dilated even with light. They are slow to react. We'll keep an eye on him and I'll take him to hospital in the morning."

By morning Carl was barely alive. During the night his condition had deteriorated and the wound on his head started bleeding again. Charlie thought it odd that he'd been with Carl in the barn that night and not noticed much blood. Later he would find it soaked into the boards under straw. But that morning Carl's head was not only bleeding, the doctor said the fracture in his skull was expanding. "I believe his brain is swelling. We have to get him to a hospital soon."

Charlie gasped in disbelief, "What, is he going to die?

Doc had wrapped Carl's head in gauze. "Honestly Charlie, I don't know. He could."

The Wilson's had purchased one of the brand new Ford Model T cars, so they reclined Carl in the back seat with Mrs. Wilson tending him until they could get him to the Beatrice Hospital.

Charlie heard the car sputter as he cranked it until the motor took the spark and began to idle making a putt putt noise. "Please take care of him. Right now I feel like he's all I have left."

Charlie sank to the ground letting go of a huge whoosh of breath. As he sat, he swore he would get the boarding house and his family back someday and Beal out of their lives.

Lula stepped out the front door as the car puttered off. "Charlie, I think you should go out and repair that ladder."

Beal stuck his head out, but Lula cut him short. "Oliver, I think the best thing is for the two of you to stay away from each other."

"Ma, I want him out of our house. Get the marriage annulled or something. That man is a menace by nature. Doc. took Carl to the hospital. He's really bad and Beal only wants me to be cheap on the lumber to repair the damage to the barn." Charlie's face pinched in pain, which unfortunately showed Beal that he had vulnerabilities. Charlie knew Beal would use it to his advantage, but he could not hide his concern for his friend.

"I know dear. I heard you and Doc loading Carl into the car. He's like another son." She reached up and kissed him on the cheek as Beal looked on. Charlie could see the anger reddening the face of his enemy and felt glad for the man's discomfort.

The rungs and sides of the ladder snapped easily under strong hands and revealed carpenter ants had riddled the wood. The pests scurried from inside the wood where they'd tunneled their way from the ground up. Curious, Charlie stomped the floor with a heel and it easily gave way. How did this hold together under my weight. My God I can't believe ants did so much damage. I didn't even notice more than one or two running around before.

Everyone already sat at the supper table as Charlie took his seat. "Ah hmm, I need everyone to listen for a moment." He waited for the quiet and continued, "Carl took a bad fall from ladder in the barn late last night. He's in Beatrice at the hospital with a fractured skull and severe concussion." An intake of breath echoed around the table.

"Is he okay, I mean will he be okay?" Roy asked his shoulders to his ears with fear.

"I don't know yet. I hope so. Most important, I've looked at the ladder and the floor boards of the barn. I'm going to have to replace a lot of it because carpenter ants riddled the wood. I don't want anyone in that barn until it's repaired. Is that clear?" He looked at the younger boys.

"What about Trotter?" Earl demanded.

Charlie couldn't help smiling at Earl. As much as he loved all his siblings, Earl was his favorite. "I checked the wood on that end of the barn too, Early B. It's in good shape and I'll only take Trotter out the back door of the barn. But, I don't want you guys in there at all. You might stumble into the bad floor and break a leg."

"Make sure the lumber and ladder you buy are inexpensive. I don't need any large expenses around this place right now. I looked at the books today. You guys spent too much money from that settlement. Things are looking good now, but no big purchases."

"I will use the lumber I need to make that barn safe for a good long time. Who do you think you are ordering us around? You have no right."

"You forget yourself, Bueller. This is Beal's Boarding House now and I want a sign that makes that clear."

"Yea Charlie, this is Mr. Beal's house now. You be nice to him." Young, impressionable Earl, Charlie's favorite brother followed Beal like a puppet.

"Earl, this man is not a friend to this house or this family."

"Beal, make your own damned sign." Charlie excused himself and apologized to the guests. He went to the barn, put the saddle and reins on the ginger colored, fifteen hands tall horse, and rode toward Beatrice. Trotter hadn't been ridden at such a pace in at least a year or more, not at a sustained run. It dawned on Charlie that the horse wheezed terribly and he slowed to a walk to let him cool. He stopped alongside the road and gave the horse some water from the ditch. It was fairly fresh rain water. Realizing how foolish he'd been by endangering the horse, he turned back. After taking care of the horse, he left it in its stall.

The remainder of the day he spent cleaning the barn floor, measuring for lumber. Somehow the loft itself didn't show any signs of damage and Charlie breathed sigh of relief.

As the day started to wane, he rolled up the cot, grabbed a bag for his clothing and kit, stepped out into the dusk and walked away.

Chapter 11 More Changes Than a Man Can Handle.

Mrs. Wilson answered his knock on their door. "Charlie, what's wrong?"

"Beal, and I'm worried about Carl. Is Doc. home?"

"Yes, he just returned before sunset. You probably passed him."

"Well, I took Trotter on the back roads to cut time, but I ran the poor animal too hard and had to turn back. Would you mind if I came in and talked to Doc?"

"No, I'm sorry I forgot my manners. Come on in and take a seat in the parlor."

It wasn't long before Dr. Wilson appeared in a chair on Charlie's right and moved close enough to lean over to pat the young man's arm. "Mama tells me you're having some trouble."

"Nothing medical, I wanted to ask about Carl. I got into a big ruckus with Beal during supper. I can't face that barn tonight and I don't want to go in the house."

"We do have an extra bedroom Charlie. You're welcome to it, right mama?"

"Most certainly," Mrs. Wilson sat a tea set on a small table and poured hot ginger tea for all of them. I'd give you coffee, but it tends to keep papa up if he drinks it this late and I think you need rest tonight as well."

"Thank you Mrs. Wilson." He looked at the doctor. "How is Carl doing? Is he going to come out of this okay?"

"He's in a coma right now Charlie, but I doubt it will last long. We found a small splinter of bone just barely sticking into his brain. The problem is that it's in the back and we never know the outcome with that. Once we opened the scalp up we could see the bone was, how can I explain this? You know what happens to a window when a rock hits it. The cracks all spread out from the center where the rock hit? Well that's sort of what happened with Carl's skull. There is some pressure from the brain swelling which is making the cracks separate just a little. Basically, it's like Carl has a big bruise in his brain. We had to be really careful removing that splinter." He paused to take a sip of tea.

"So, he still has a chance?"

"Oh of course, I'm sorry. I just wanted to give you an explanation of his condition that you can understand. We have to wait for the swelling to go down. The coma is a good thing really because he's not fussing around and causing it to swell more. Once that's down he should wake up and we'll see if he has any loss of memory, speech, movement or anything." Doc Wilson stopped for a breath and put a hand on his young friend's shoulder. "We just don't know with the brain what will happen. There are doctors starting to study it, but most of it is by situation and autopsies. There is the new x ray, but only the biggest university hospitals have those. They do the studies." He took another sip of his tea then handed it over to his wife to heat up. "Anyway, I do go on when I talk about this stuff. The most important thing we can do is be patient and let Carl rest. If the swelling is starting to go down by tomorrow, we'll have a better idea of how soon he'll wake up. Does that help?"

Charlie sat listening intently, wanting to flop back with a huge sigh of relief, but he'd have to accept that there was nothing certain about Carl's outcome. "Thanks for letting me know. I guess we'll just have to bide our time. I hate that, but if it's all I can do that's it. Could I go see him."

"Why don't you wait until he wakes up, which I'm sure he will, until then let's let him rest.

"Alright Dr. Wilson, I don't know what our family would do without you."

"What else is bothering you?"

"I checked the barn and there are carpenter ants all over the front end especially near the ladder and even in the ladder itself. I don't know how it didn't fall apart under my weight." He handed his empty cup to Mrs. Wilson, holding his hand out to let her know he didn't want more.

"What was the blow up with Beal about?"

"The cost of lumber, he wants me to use the cheapest there is, and the cheapest possible ladder. He's been through our books and insists he's in charge of Beal's Boarding House now. He even ordered me to make a sign." Charlie could feel the muscles in his neck tensing and his heart throbbing. "I'm sorry, I get kind of wound up."

"You had an idea that might happen. I mean about Beal taking over."

"Knowing it doesn't make it easier. But, I'm going to get the proper lumber for that barn so that it has a strong floor, and I'm getting an oak ladder."

"I don't blame you. If you need any help with the expense, I'm sure I can find some work for you to do here and I'll help with the expense of your barn."

"Doc. do you know how many people would tell you you're crazy to deal with a dark man?"

The older man laughed. "Do you think I care? They all need me when they have a sliver." Then they were both caught up in the fun as the clock chimed eleven times. The chime seemed like a cue for the doctor to yawn, and Charlie followed suit. He looked to see if Mrs. Wilson yawned as well.

"Doc smiled. You missed her. She left a couple minutes ago. "She's used to being the nurse when I have a patient stay here. I have one room for a patient. She treads very softly." He chuckled, stood and patted Charlie's shoulder. "I'll show you your room."

Chapter 12: Moving On

Charlie never returned to the now Beal Boarding House. He purchased the lumber with his winnings from poker and a donation from Dr. Wilson. With a safe, pine board, barn floor and oak ladder, an occasional visit and outings with the children made for his contact with his family. Lula searched him out one day and found him alone doing repairs in the barn..

"Charlie?"

"Oh, Hi mother,' he looked up for a moment and continued nailing the floor boards into place.

"Son, I'm so sorry. I really didn't believe he could be so horrible. I should have listened and now..."

He didn't look up, the tightness of her voice revealed her tears; there was no need to embarrass her more by making a deal of it. Once she had a minute to compose herself, Charlie put the hammer down and sat on a bale looking at her.

"Ma, I overplayed my hand too soon. I didn't want it to come to this. Honestly, I hoped I was wrong, but Fred got back too late."

"I know. We didn't tell you about the rush on the wedding because Oliver wanted to avoid more friction and thought when it was over, you'd see him as a good guy who loves your family. I thought he was sincere." She shook her head. "At least he treats the younger children well."

"I know you can't undo it or you'll lose the house. Besides the kids need stability, there's been too many loses in the last five years."

"Is there any way you will come back and live here, even in the barn?"

"I don't think so. Carl and I are just over at the Wilson's. They assumed I'd be staying on for a while, and I'm grateful. I'm not far so you and the kids can see me just about any time." He reached over and took her hand in his. There was such warmth emanating from her it seemed to travel up his arm, down his chest and straight to his heart. "Carl is out of the hospital as of yesterday. Doc's keeping him in his patient room attached to the clinic. It's amazing how they built all that. The house doesn't look so huge by comparison to ours, but the three bedrooms are all along one wall upstairs with a hall that leads down from the bedrooms to the clinic. Doc. keeps their room right above the patient room. He's even got a vent between them so he hears anything that happens and Mrs. Wilson is his nurse. Doc. trained her himself so that she is able to do almost anything needed while doc sleeps if there is a patient in residence. It's like a small hospital in a clinic, attached to the house and looks like all one home from the outside, except for the Dr.'s shingle of course."

Lula visibly bounced on the bale where she sat. "Charlie, you seem so happy. I haven't heard you so excited in a long time. Do you remember when you and Pa brought all of us home to the boarding house when you were just a boy?"

"Yes, I do remember that. I loved helping pa build this place. I jumped up and down when we first brought the family here. I ran you around trying to show you every nail I'd hammered." His voice lifted as he acted out fond memories of that day.

Lula stood up and laughed at his antics. "I know and that's how you sound now. Son, I hope you find a place building things." Her head dropped. "Unfortunately, I found out too late that Mr. Beal is a destroyer."

"I talked to Jack and Roy and if I'm not around they are going to make sure Beal doesn't wreck this family."

"I hope that isn't necessary." She hugged his muscular arm. "How is Carl? Does he have any brain damage, or paralysis? Can he remember things?"

"He's got some work to do. His speech is a little slurred, but he walks fine and the only thing he doesn't remember is the day of the fall. I think that's a blessing. His muscles are a little weak so we're all working to make him do exercises, and Mrs. Wilson has him speaking better every day. Mostly he just has to retrain his tongue on a few sounds." A smile crept across the brown face. "Mother, he's so resilient. I don't know what I would do if I lost the only true friend I've ever had."

"I've known Carl long enough to learn he's very special. He's almost my tenth child." She laughed at herself.

Even if Charlie didn't really get the joke, he was glad to see her joy.

Over the following weeks gambling became Charlie's biggest source of income. He liked gambling. It was the one thing he had the most control over in his life. Poker gave him the comfort of escape. The poker table only saw a third of his winnings from one day to the next. The rest he hid in a jar. He helped do some repairs for the Wilson's to pay back for the five dollars they loaned for the barn. Carl worked alongside him getting stronger every day.

The snow fell outside in an opaque soft curtain of white. Charlie thought, *two days to the New Year, just two days to the beginning of a new decade.* Charlie felt ready.

"Carl, would you like to go with me to Omaha?"

Three people at the dinner table looked up from their soup. "What?"

"I had a letter from Fred. He's invited me to come to Omaha."

"Okay Charlie, but I want to ko to St. Joseph." Carl still had difficulty with the soft g sound. It came out as a guttural k.

"St. Joseph, what's in St. Joseph?"

"It's where I krew up. We can find work there. I want to build."

"Charlie, I think you should consider Carl's idea. Omaha will be good fun with Fred, but you know he'll be moving on with his boxing.

I've heard he's getting some wins." Doc punched at the air a couple of times.

"Papa, stop that before you spill everyone's soup."

"Sorry."

They all looked at Charlie until he answered. "Okay, if Carl wants to go to St. Joseph, that's fine. I'd like to go to Omaha and from there I don't know what I want to do."

"Okay, I'll ko to Omaha with you for a little while, then I'm koing to St. Joseph. I need to work. You should work too Charlie. Kambling isn't for living."

"I know it's an uncertain living, but I'm smart about it."

"You do what you think is right." Carl nodded.

"Wait now," Mrs. Wilson spoke up. "You can't just decide you're going to leave and have no more plans than that Charlie. You are a good carpenter, why don't you work with Carl on that. You boys have been friends for a long time now."

"Mama, it's his decision."

"I'm very grateful to all of you. I might go to St. Joseph and work. My life seems out of control. Beal took almost everything away." Charlie walked to the window as his baritone voice raised in pitch and volume from his internal battle. "It's not that easy."

"But it is that easy Charlie." Doc spoke up. "I'm not saying you give up, just make a decision to do something and see if it works. Most of us don't know about tomorrow we think we do. You may find yourself a whole new life."

"Besides, you haven't lost your family." Mrs. Wilson said. "Your mother is still across the street, your brothers are there. Don't be a coward and let Beal take you out of the family. You know that's exactly what he wants."

Carl didn't say anymore, he just nodded.

"Give me time. I know my ma still loves me and my brothers Jack and Roy are still there for me. Beal has a big hold on little Earl." He rubbed the back of his head. "Let's just go to Omaha and then I'll decide if I want to go to St. Joseph with you. Okay Carl?"

"Okay for now."

"You do know you're always welcome in our home don't you Charlie? You're at home here too Carl. Mrs. Wilson and I love having you both here."

"Yes Charlie." Mrs. Wilson spoke up. "We've never told you, but Papa and I feel your family is our family. We never had any children of our own. We've watched you all grow up. Please don't leave us all without knowing there is still a lot of love for you here Charlie, in this house and in your home."

"Thank you for that Mrs. Wilson. I guess we feel that you're part of our family too. I just never thought about it that way." He stood and looked out the window at a house five room long, two rooms deep and two full stories tall. He knew because he'd helped build it. "The boarding house isn't my home anymore."

"As long as your mother is there, Charlie, it is your home base. We all grow up and leave home one way or another. It's your time to move on." Mrs. Wilson kissed him on the cheek. "Now grow up and be a man. Go forth and find your niche in the world."

Charlie kissed her back. "Carl, what do you say, shall I follow you this time and find my niche."

Carl laughed. "I think for now, let's just get moving."

About The Author

G. K. Fralin a dyed in the woods and waters of Kansas, Blue River rat now resides in Southeast Nebraska with her husband of over thirty seven years.

I loved growing up under the protection of the Flint Hills in walking distance of the Big Blue River. The scenic majesty of that valley plays heavily into my work.

I moved to Nebraska, only forty five minutes north of the farm I grew up on, and married the love of my life. We raised three children, and have ten grandchildren.

As you can see family, my country background, conservative Christian values and my vivid imagination all play into what I write. As well as do things I learned through 20 years of working in nursing caring for people with special needs, those needing skilled nursing care and so forth. I may not use specific individuals, but many of my characters take on the personalities or features of people I know.

My first book <u>The Search</u> follows a young author trapped in a small town off Interstate 80, in Nebraska. Once there she can't get out the way she came in. The innkeeper becomes increasingly disturbing to the point of sinister undertones. The few town people talk about Shepherd who will be returning and is the only one who can lead her through the treacherous journey out of the small town of Hidden.

My second book consists of a selection of short stories titled <u>Six Strange Short Stories</u>.

I am a member of the Nebraska Writer's Guild that consists of wonderful authors willing to encourage and lend bits of advice and opportunities to meet with other writers.

Excerpts from other books by G. K. Fralin

https://www.smashwords.com/books/view/242817

The Search

Chapter 1

Sheridan woke up alongside a country road where a thick late afternoon fog forced her off the highway the evening before. The unseasonable blinding whiteness was eerie, but not unheard of in Nebraska.

The mist took over so quickly the exit almost disappeared from view before she turned onto a Nebraska back road. She'd been headed to a book signing for her novel "Living Bedouin."

She wiped the sleep from her eyes. Every muscle stiff and sore, even with her slight five foot four inch frame, curling up in the back seat of her minivan made her feel cramped.

Peeling her sticky, thick tongue from the roof of her mouth made the icky taste even more like rotten food. She fished through her bag for a bottle of water. Finding it, she swished some around in her mouth then opened the window to spit into the heavy fog.

Reading the map, she determined she must be within miles to LIncoln. The fog hadn't lifted. In fact, it was probably denser than the night before. She checked for a signal on her cell phone again, but she was in a dead zone and even the GPS wouldn't target a position. She would have to call Michael once back on Interstate 80.

She smiled at the thought of Michael. After three years of mourning the death of her husband, Mark, she was finally dating again. Michael had encouraged her to finish her doctorate in anthropology.

For over a month, Sheridan toured Nebraska, Kansas, Iowa, and Missouri promoting and doing book signings for her book based upon her doctoral thesis.

Along the way, she stopped in small towns and found church groups and other small town meetings. She set a goal of writing a book about the local communities, from the history of their founders, to the present day remnants of those roots.

The people were hospitable and their community strength often centered on church and family. The differences that seeped into their present day lives were their unique ancestral histories. With more research, most of which she could do from home, another book would soon be off to the publisher.

Sheridan loved her position with the university, and probably published enough to keep her on faculty. The idea of giving up the writing and particularly the research sickened her. Field research was the most fun.

The glaze of fixed concentration cleared from her mind and she could see the fog lifted. A few feet in front of her, an old, painted, wooden sign read Hidden 1/2 mile. The sign made her laugh, "Oh why not" she said aloud. It would probably take about a day to research one more town and it might put a nice ending to the new book.

First, Sheridan attempted a three point turn on the narrow road to point her car back toward Interstate 80.

The fog bank became denser as she made the turn and felt her tires start to slide over the edge of a ditch. She managed to pull forward, safely back onto the road.

Shaking uncontrollably, Sheridan left the car to walk the half mile to Hidden.

Looking back toward the signpost, the fog had completely cleared. She looked behind her into an opaque white curtain. A shiver ran down her back as she walked the half mile into town. Looking back a few times the strange thick fog seemed to follow her. All landmarks disappeared one by one. She felt as if some sinister force was following her, pushing her toward Hidden.

A huge Victorian mansion greeted her immediately when stepping into the town. The huge double doors were wide enough for three or four men side by side to walk through.

A sign at the corner read simply 'Street'. She stood back and looked at it again trying to find the outline of faded letters or numbers in front of the word. There weren't any. There really wasn't room for anything but the word Street.

Stepping onto the wooden sidewalk in front of the building, she turned to look across to the other side of Street. *Oh, ho ho, this town is going to be very interesting.* She took a slow three hundred sixty degree turn and saw it was the only visible street. She didn't see any alleys. However, footpaths broke up what she considered city blocks.

She looked down and noticed she stood in the middle of the street. *I must have twirled or something.*

Everything around her started spinning. There was a bench in front of the Victorian and she tottered toward it. As soon as she took her first step back toward the Inn, the dizziness was gone.

Okay, this is getting super weird. She threw the thought away deciding the dizziness was due to lack of decent sleep.

Sheridan turned her attention back toward the Inn.

From her vantage point in the middle of Street, she could see the long wings spreading from each side of the central section. The well maintained, ancient building loomed imposing over the street.

Standing in front of the great walnut doors again, she noticed the left door had a large bronze knocker shaped like a flower that was obviously out of some artist's abstract mind. The other door boasted a matching bronze plaque, "Hide Inn: Come on In."

She ran her finger over the bronze flower and was shocked that it seemed softer than most bronzes. It was like bronzed baby shoes. She could feel the feathery shape of the petals and even striations of a feather. The grouping of petals was not unlike a lily. The abstract rendition reminded her of a painting she had in her living room of a rose bud in a vase that upon second look was a woman's hand.

The stem of the bronze flower made up the knocker and clanged like a heavy weight against its back plate. Sheridan jumped in shock as she heard the noise reverberate through the interior of the great building.

As she waited, Sheridan looked across and down the street. All the buildings were limestone. Limestone quarries dotted the plains so it wasn't surprising. What did puzzle her was the buildings were all the same square design, except one.

The limestone across the street looked like a church of some kind. It had a sign standing in the yard with the words Angel Choir Chapel. The Chapel boasted a bell tower, but no visible doors

Why would anybody build a church with no front door? The curiosity of the researcher determined to discover the essence of the tiny town.

She suddenly realized there wasn't another soul visible. *So sad, another small Nebraska ghost town.* She sniffed the air. It was clean, like after a rain. No, it was cleaner. There were no farm smells, no alfalfa, animal feces, or fuel odors.

She slapped the back of her hand when she felt a sting and thought comically that they must have forgotten to take the insects.

A feeling of deep calm washed over her. She didn't know why, but she didn't want to question it. She almost felt drugged, like after taking a pain pill.

I really need some sleep before I fall over. She rubbed her arms and patted her cheeks. "Oh My." The words spread into a wide yawn.

She stretched her arms out and took a deep breath of the fresh air. The feeling of relaxation continued down her entire body as she inhaled the crispness deep into her lungs. She began to feel hazy and a little wobbly.

Then something else filled the air.

Sheridan felt goose bumps rise on her arms as she noticed a faint, melody. It had been there unnoticed since her arrival. It was like having the radio in her car on very low and suddenly noticing the music.

The sounds were the most beautiful harmony of voices she'd ever heard. It came from inside the chapel across the street. They sounded like a combination of halleluiahs, with an undertone of humming. Her heart lifted and warmth washed through her body. She wanted to go find the singer's but turned when she heard a movement behind her.

Methuselah opened the door of the Inn. The short, odd, little man looked like he bore the wisdom of the nearly 1000 year old man from the Biblical comparison. Each crater like wrinkle seemed to disappear when he smiled.

"Good morning young lady. Me thinks you have a problem with reading."

His gravely voice belied the youthful agility he displayed with a funny little jump and kick that reminded her of a leprechaun. He pointed to the sign on the door.

"I'm sorry sir, I couldn't resist the knocker. I've never seen anything like it."

"He's a curious flower, he is for sure." The old man's phrasing was so quaint she would have to make note of it to use in her book. He would make an interesting figure.

His face furrowed with deep wrinkles. His thick, wavy, gray hair nicely trimmed with a full, well groomed beard. The man was somewhat stooped, but she noticed he stood erect very easily.

She enjoyed his theatrics, but wondered just how much she could trust the old guy. She tried to gauge his height compared by her own. She guessed him to be a few inches taller.

The odd, little innkeeper didn't fit the majestic feel of the Inn.

"Well I can see you are going to be an interesting guest."

"Excuse me?"

As he motioned her through the door, he enlightened her. "I've learned two things about you already. You don't follow instructions and you can't fight temptation." His smile grew from ear to ear with what she assumed was some sense of self satisfaction

As he lifted his left hand to welcome her inside, she noticed it was a child sized hand. It looked smooth and soft. His right hand was a man's hand, rough and calloused from hard work.

"I see you've discovered my gifted hands." He held them both up.

"You sir, are a wonder." Sheridan laughed the words more than stated them, which seemed to encourage him.

He led Sheridan to a large bureau made of cherry wood in a lobby at the end of a long, wide corridor. She noticed doors to rooms off both sides of the passageway. One door was open revealing an office. She imagined the other doors were equally utilitarian, except one labeled in great polished brass letters: SHEPHERD'S CLOSET.

Once they entered the lobby, their voices echoed and Sheridan looked up to see all the way to the top of the three story building with grand staircases curving up to each wing from the base. She felt that she must try to sketch it, however rough her talent.

She stood at the bureau and pulled out her credit card. The old man slapped a ledger on its top. "I just need a room for one day. I only plan to stay for a good nap and let the fog lift. That is the weirdest fog down the road."

"What fog? It looks clear enough to me."

"That's what makes it so odd. It's clear as a bell in this direction, but every time I'd try to turn back toward the highway, I was in the deep fog again."

"Not to worry young lady."

He doesn't believe me.

He turned the book in her direction and glanced at the card. "Take things for granted too I see. You don't pay until you leave. The cost of your stay depends on what you do with your time here." Before she could grab it, he picked up her card, pulled out a large pair of scissors, and chopped it into four pieces.

"WHAT THE HECK DO YOU THINK YOU'RE DOING? YOU HAD NO RIGHT. I WANT A PHONE SO I CAN CALL MY FRIEND IN LINCOLN."

She took a deep breath. *Was the man deaf?* He continued what he was doing as if she'd said nothing.

"HEY" Sheridan grabbed his arm. "Phone"

"Heard ya, don't have one"

"So, if you don't want money, how do I get you to find me a phone and get me the heck out of here? Do I have to clean the Inn or help paint the church?" The sarcasm seemed lost on the host. *This cat and mouse game is over.*

"If I have to take a chance walking back to the interstate, I will."

"Nope, Sheridan Easterly," was all he said. His eyes twinkled like a child playing gotcha. She could see the game was still on. "Oh, by the way, trying to walk back out of here would be a big risk. You'll just get turned around again and again and end up back here anyway."

"What is this place?"

"It's Hidden. Didn't you read the sign?"

Sheridan looked down at the ledger. It lay open to a clean page. It looked brand new, as did the pen that lay on top of it. The pen was a quill and the bottle of ink sat on the desktop next to the ledger along with a clean cloth for letting the excess ink drip before signing.

"It fits, it looks perfect for the Inn. I'll sign so I can get a nap, but I will be leaving as soon as that fog lifts." She signed her name in a Romanesque calligraphy, which was odd because she never studied the art.

He grabbed her large tote bag and waved his arm like a scoop signaling her to a grand staircase. "Practical woman, you travel light."

"Nothing much escapes you does it?" *Who is this idiot?*

"That's why they call me Catch."

Sheridan sighed. "I've traveled a lot   Catch"

"That's what everybody calls me. I like it. Keeps me mysterious ya know?"

"Catch" She repeated. "And I suppose you think you've caught me in this tiny ghost town. I'll take a nap, but then I will go back down that road." There was more determination in her voice than in her mind.

"Did you know that your name, Sheridan, means to search? Are you a searcher, Sheridan?"

The old man had a bad habit of ignoring her no matter how angry she spat words at him.

He carried her tote up an ornate staircase. "Yes, I do know what my name means. How did you know my name? You called me by my name before I even signed your ledger."

"Tsk, tsk, little lady, You'll raise your blood pressure.

He pointed to an identity tag on her tote.

"Oh, that works too." A deep yawn escaped her as he opened the door to her room. "I guess I'm more tired than I thought. It's ridiculous to think you are keeping me prisoner. I will have to report that card stolen you know. You are in big trouble. That's frowned upon in Nebraska, you know."

"Okay." He said nothing else about it, just the one word, okay. *Does this man think he's untouchable?*

Sheridan noticed symbols on a wall plaque beside the door. "What is this all about?" Sheridan pointed to the plaque. "It looks like some kind of ancient, symbolic script."

She traced the symbols lightly with her fingers. The contrast of stiff, dry balsa wood against the smooth, polished wood of the door jam oddly seemed to fit. The symbols seemed familiar. "Hmm," She became the scientist again. "These symbols look like an ancient lost language. I've seen something like them somewhere."

"Well, it probably is authentic then." Catch opened the door.

Sheridan peered into the room and gasped.

The contrast overwhelmed her. The new Early American style furnishings of the suite took her by surprise. The bathroom door stood open revealing all the gadgets of the most elegant hotels.

She made her way to the bathroom door and saw a walk in, tiled shower, a large vanity complete with ornate mirror, built in hair dryer and plush rug.

The bathtub was large enough for two with body massaging jets. "Wow, this is something that I plan to take advantage of right away." She turned and smiled back at Catch. There were even bottles of her favorite brands of shampoo, lavender soaps, and candles setting on top of the marble counter.

Sheridan suddenly remembered the violation Catch perpetrated on her property.

The old man smiled, "Ye didn't think we were all backward did ye?" Catch seemed to have an endless repertoire of wisecracks to suit his chosen persona. He even added a hitch in his git a long to go with the old hillbilly.

Catch deposited the tote on a bench in a spacious closet.

"This doesn't make up for the card you destroyed."

"Expired"

"Expired? I have until the end of the month before it expires."

"Close enough."

"You're not talking so cocky now. Are you a little scared?"

"Ha, hardly"

Sheridan's energy drained so she had none left for arguing.

Looking around the room, Sheridan noticed a large portrait of the same odd flower as on the doorknocker. The room was like a dream from her youth. The color scheme and design of the room were in her favorite colors and styles.

Thinking of finally getting a chance to call Michael, she noticed there was no phone, television, or even a radio.

"Mr. Catch, I'd hoped for a telephone to call my friend in Lincoln. I don't see any in the room."

"No need to be so formal, just call me Catch." He drew in a breath. "We live simple here. We don't use phones, cars, or any of the things that make the world move so fast out there in the world."

"Don't you have a telephone downstairs for emergencies?"

"I'm afraid it isn't working, and I don't know when it'll be fixed. We have an old two way radio. I'll see if we can get that to work." Catch replied. "You should get some rest and something to eat. You aren't expected today are you?"

"No, not particularly, my friend is used to me not checking in for a day or two. This isn't the first spot I've been in where I couldn't get a signal." *Why did I tell him that? Its not exactly information you give to someone you don't trust.*

Catch started to leave the room then looked back. "You are here because you are supposed to be here." He said almost in a whisper as he started out the door.

"What does that mean?"

He kept walking down the hall.

"WHAT DOES THAT MEAN?"

"Enjoy your room, you will find everything you need."

"Wait, don't I get a key?"

"No need for them around here." The old man turned his back to her and continued on his way.

Sheridan was alone in a lavish room, done up as if they decorated it exclusively for her. "How odd" She made a deep sigh and looked around the room.

A chair at the little table fit perfectly under the doorknob. "There"

A bath sent warm relaxation through her body. The water gently rolled over each part as she twisted and nearly swam in luxury.

Stepping out on the rug her feet sank so deep her it tickled the top of her feet. In the closet, a robe of pink silk slid over her body like a caress.

Sheridan forgot her fears, her anger, her frustration and fell into that welcome calm she'd felt when she first arrived.

The flower portrait on the wall detailed more of the subject. The leaves were heart shaped with red veins. The petals were feathery and white. The artist had painted a yellow gold stamen as if it shown like burnished gold.

She was curious about the designer who could have dreamed up such a beautiful theme for the Hide Inn.

Without thinking, Sheridan found herself sniffing at the painting as if she'd inhale the fragrance of the flower. Oddly enough, she found it smelled like a freshly cut lilac that the painter must have mixed into the paint.

She pulled her laptop from it's tote and filled two pages of her journal. Her report was a mess of the day's events. She started doubting her own impressions of the innkeeper. Maybe the card had expired. She typed it all into her notes and set it aside for her return to Lincoln. She concluded with a note to Michael so she'd remember to tell him how she cared for him before hitting him with the craziness of that day.

Sheridan loved Michael and she knew he loved her. Their love was companionable rather than electric but just as heart felt and deep.

Her eyes drooped and soon she was nodding off in the desk chair. Her stomach groaned in protest, so she a banana from the immense fruit and cheese basket on the table by the sofa, then slid between the silk sheets of the huge soft bed. As she tried to think through the muddle of circumstances, she drifted in and out until the day gave way to slumber.

https://www.smashwords.com/books/view/212395

Six Strange Short Stories

Dust Short Excerpt

Sweat dripped into her eyes faster than she could wipe her brow. Temperatures over 100 degrees made the air conditioning nearly useless. The one half mile drive home on the dirt road caused Theresa Finch to second guess their decision to buy the small acreage on the dusty road.

Without warning, a gust sprayed dirt and debris onto her windshield. The car rocked as the winds picked up speed. Just a little farther, Theresa thought. She had seen the house not far ahead before the dust storm blinded her path. She fought to steer to the right and searched for landmarks, in particular the house that had just disappeared from view.

She heard a bump as the car lurched slightly backward. A brief scream filled her ears as her front tires crept over a lumpy object. The back tires mounted and rolled off the obstacle. There was an awful noise of tearing and bumping underneath the vehicle before the car stopped. *Breath, Theresa Breath. Her pulse throbbed in her ears.*

She knew she had run over a person. No animal made a terrorizing scream like that.

"Oh, dear God," she pleaded, as her head turned instinctively upward.

The car door violently pushed back by the weight of the wind. Covering her nose and mouth with the front of her shirt, she fought her way out. One hand feeling along the car,

She swept her foot back and forth to find what she couldn't see through the thick, dusty air.

Then her foot nudged something soft. She reached her hand down and felt a still body about two feet long. She felt cloth, skin, "Alana, please not Alana" she begged.

(read the rest of this and other stories in Six Strange Short Stories by G. K. Fralin)

https://www.smashwords.com/profile/view/GKFralin

https://www.facebook.com/GKFralin

http://www.gkfralinbooks.blogspot.com

https://twitter.com/GKFralin

http://www.wordsprings.blogspot.com

http://www.linkedin.com

Search linkedin for G. K. Fralin (the link is too long for this publication)

We are all remarkable, unique individuals. Celbrate what makes you different. Thank you for reading the first instalment of the Charlie Bueller Series.

G. K. Fralin

Printed in Great Britain
by Amazon